Science Behind Sports

# Lacrosse

## Science on the Field

By Gary Wiener

LUCENT PRESS

Published in 2018 by
**Lucent Press, an Imprint of Greenhaven Publishing, LLC**
353 3rd Avenue
Suite 255
New York, NY 10010



Designer: Seth Hughes
Editor: Vanessa Oswald

**Cataloging-in-Publication Data**

Names: Wiener, Gary.
Title: Lacrosse: Science on the Field / Gary Wiener.
Description: New York : Lucent Press, 2018. | Series: Science behind sports | Includes index.
Identifiers: ISBN 9781534561175 (library bound) | ISBN 9781534561182 (ebook)
Subjects: LCSH: Lacrosse–Juvenile literature.
Classification: LCC GV989.14 W54 2018 | DDC 796.36'2–dc23

Printed in the United States of America

CPSIA compliance information: Batch #BS17KL: For further information contact Greenhaven Publishing LLC, New York, New York at 1-844-317-7404.

Please visit our website, www.greenhavenpublishing.com. For a free color catalog of all our high-quality books, call toll free 1-844-317-7404 or fax 1-844-317-7405.

# Contents

# Foreword

When people watch a sporting event, they often say things such as, "That was unbelievable!" or "How could that happen?" The achievements of superstar athletes often seem humanly impossible—as if they defy the laws of nature—and all sports fans can seemingly do is admire them in awe.

However, when a person learns the science behind sports, the unbelievable becomes understandable. It no longer seems as if athletes at the top of their game are defying the laws of nature to achieve greatness; it seems as if they are using the laws of nature to their fullest potential. This kind of knowledge might be thought by some to take away from a pure appreciation of sports, but that is far from the truth. Understanding the science that makes athletic achievements possible allows fans to gain an even deeper appreciation for athletic performances and how athletes use science to their advantage.

This series introduces readers to the scientific principles behind some of the world's most popular sports. As they learn about physics concepts such as acceleration, gravity, and kinetic versus potential energy, they discover how these concepts can be applied to pitches in baseball, flips in gymnastics, dunks in basketball, and other movements in a variety of sports. In addition to the physics behind amazing plays, readers discover the science behind basic training and conditioning for different sports, the biology involved in understanding common sports injuries and their treatments, and the technological advances paving the way for the future of athletics.

The scientific concepts presented in this series are explained using accessible language and engaging examples. Complicated principles are simplified through the use of detailed diagrams, charts, graphs, and a helpful glossary. Quotations from scientists, athletes, and coaches give readers a firsthand perspective, and further research is encouraged through a detailed bibliography and a list of additional resources.

Athletes, sports fans, and budding scientists will get something important out of this series: information about how to exercise and fuel the body to excel in competition, a deeper appreciation for the history of their favorite sport, and a stronger understanding of how science works in the world around us.

The worlds of science and sports are not as far apart as they may seem. In fact, sports could not exist without science. In understanding the relationship between these two worlds, readers will become more knowledgeable sports fans and better athletes.

Chapter 1

# The Fastest Game on Two Feet

It was a hot August afternoon in Western New York. Under a bright sun, a group of players, ranging from 13 to 60 years old, engaged in a lacrosse scrimmage on a high school field surrounded by bleachers. There was no one in the stands. The players tossed the ball expertly from one to another, and it rarely hit the ground unless a shot was attempted. One of the players was just entering high school, several were college students, some were ex-college players who now participate just for fun, and others were nearing retirement age. Players rotated in and out, with midfielders sometimes spending only a few minutes out on the field, trying to avoid heat exhaustion. One midfielder intercepted the ball on the defensive end, then sprinted the length of the field toward the opposing goalie. As he neared the net, in one swift movement, he brought the lacrosse stick behind his shoulders and flipped the ball past the goalie into the net. The other players called him "Hollywood."

These two dozen players in an empty stadium were playing "The Creator's Game." Whether they participated to increase their skills or for sheer enjoyment, they all share the same passion for this ancient sport. At its heart, lacrosse is a simple game. As one former player, Sean Lydon, remarked when asked to describe the sport, "Put the rubber ball in the big metal square. Hit people. Run a lot. Repeat."[1] However, like any endeavor, lacrosse is also so much more. "A game of constant action and exceptional grace," Johns Hopkins coach David Pietramala wrote, "[it] combines the individual skill of baseball, the physical demands of football, the team strategies of basketball, and the conditioning required in soccer."[2]

*Many play lacrosse simply for the enjoyment of the sport.*

## Native American Origins

Like the blues and jazz in music and the short story in literature, lacrosse is a uniquely North American invention. The blues originates with African Americans, and the short story began with American author Edgar Allan Poe, who first defined it. Lacrosse goes back much further, to the original inhabitants of America—the Native Americans—who played the game centuries before Europeans ever set eyes on the North American continent.

## Fast Break!

Early lacrosse had virtually no rules against rough play, and because players wore no protective gear, they often finished a game bruised and bloodied.

Lacrosse was a widely popular activity among Native Americans. It was played by at least 48 Native American groups in southern Canada and in all parts of the United States other than the extreme Southwest. Lacrosse "was of tremendous importance to the Indians"[3] and performed many functions: It was a spiritual game, dubbed "The Creator's Game," as it was often thought of as a gift from a higher power; it could be used to settle disputes, such as disputes over land; it was a recreational game that fostered brotherhood and community among its players; and it was also a war game that enabled warriors to keep in shape and mimicked many of the activities of warfare. So central was this last function that "in native languages of southeastern tribes lacrosse was called 'brother to war,' or 'little brother of war,' and most historians writing on the sport stressed its violent nature."[4]

Early lacrosse had many such names, as each tribe had its own term for the sport. The Algonquin group called it *teiontsesiksaheks*; the Haudenosaunee name was *tehontshikSaheks*. However, the most common name Native Americans used was *baggataway*. Primitive lacrosse was dramatically different from that which is seen today on high school, college, and professional fields. It was a mass game, with teams rarely having fewer than 100 players and sometimes having more than 1,000. The playing field could be miles long (although most were under 0.5 mile, or 0.8 km), and games could last for days. There was no prescribed width to the playing field, so play could range far and near. Some tribes "used a single pole or tree or rock" for the goal, and players scored by hitting the target with the ball. "Others had two goal posts, six to nine feet apart, and the ball had to pass between them."[5] Players often wore only breechcloth and generally went barefoot.

All of these features helped promote the strength, endurance, and teamwork of tribal warriors. As Donald M. Fisher wrote, "Because war was a constant threat, native people placed a great emphasis on military power and diplomacy. The most obvious purpose of a ball game was to sustain a nation by keeping its men strong and healthy for war and hunting. The constant running, rough play, and stick skills need[ed] to play the game conditioned men for combat."[6] In some cases, if a player slowed down and could not keep up with the others, "squaws from his tribe ran on the field, and beat him into showing more activity."[7]

*Early lacrosse was a mass game, with participants sometimes numbering more than 1,000.*

## European Interest

An example of the militaristic use of lacrosse occurred on June 4, 1763, when the Ojibway (also called Chippewa) and Sac Native Americans arranged a demonstration lacrosse game to be played for the benefit of English soldiers to commemorate the birthday of King George III. The match was held just outside the walls of Fort Mackinac in upper Michigan. The English happily enjoyed the spectacle, even betting on the outcome, until the players launched the ball over the walls of the fort, followed the projectile inside, and proceeded to slaughter the inhabitants, thus taking control of the fort.

Europeans had taken an interest in *baggataway* seemingly from the moment they first learned of the game. Jesuit missionary Jean de Brébeuf saw the Hurons playing the game near Thunder Bay in Ontario, Canada, in 1636, and first applied the word *crosse* to the sport in a report to his superiors in France. The sticks that the Native Americans used "looked like the crosier (*la crosse*), which is the staff that bishops carry in religious ceremonies."[8] The name stuck.

Legend has it that a group of French pioneers may have been the first to play the Native Americans at their own game in 1740. However, there are no records of any contests involving Europeans until almost a full century later; generally speaking, Europeans "viewed the sports and pastimes of the Indians with tolerant amusement."[9] It was in the mid-1800s that lacrosse began to take hold among the non-natives, and it did so first in Canada.

## Canadian Innovations

In the 1840s, a young Canadian, William George Beers, became infatuated with lacrosse. As a teenager in the 1850s, he joined the Montreal Lacrosse Club, the first organized white team to play the game. Beers would go on to

## Box Lacrosse

Box Lacrosse, or indoor lacrosse—often simply called box—was born when Canadian promoters were seeking a way to fill up empty ice hockey arenas during the off-season. It has grown in popularity and has led to the formation of professional leagues, most notably the National Lacrosse League (NLL). As of 2016, the NLL had nine teams—five in the United States and four in Canada.

The object of box lacrosse is the same as that of field lacrosse, which is to put the ball in the goal. However, box lacrosse is a faster game, due to the smaller field (the size of an ice hockey rink) and, in the NLL, a 30-second shot clock, which begins counting down as soon as a team gains possession of the ball. Only six players per team compete at any one time, and a great deal of body contact is permitted in the tight playing area.

The indoor surface may be bare concrete, though at higher levels, the playing area is generally covered by artificial turf. Players who enjoy field lacrosse may find box to be an exciting alternative when it is too cold to play outdoors.

have a successful career as a dentist, but he would also be instrumental in growing the game of lacrosse. In 1867, he formed the Canadian National Lacrosse Association. In this year, lacrosse exploded in Canada: "On June 1, there were only six [Canadian lacrosse] clubs in Canada; by the end of the year there were eighty."[10]

Each club had its own rules, and so games were preceded by "a certain amount of diplomatic negotiation."[11] However, in June of that year, Beers laid down the first set of rules for organized lacrosse. Beers was a proponent of the team game, so his rules favored that style over individual play. In 1869, he published the first book about the sport, entitled *Lacrosse: The National Game of Canada*.

Canadians have always been innovators in the lacrosse game. Box lacrosse, the indoor version of the sport, was developed in the 1930s in Canada. In 1931, Canadian arena owners formed the International Lacrosse League, which featured four teams: the Montreal Canadiens, the Montreal Maroons, the Toronto Maple Leafs, and the Cornwall Colts.

Shown here is an early lacrosse team in their uniforms.

## The United States Discovers Lacrosse

Also in 1867, a group of Native Americans demonstrated the sport for white Americans in Saratoga Springs, New York. "This event brought the first mention of lacrosse in ... American newspapers."[12] The first game in New York City occurred a year later. The *New York Tribune* stated that "Lacrosse may be called a madman's game, so wild it is."[13] Intercollegiate lacrosse, which for over a century, has been the lifeblood of the sport, began with men's play in 1877. The first intercollegiate game was between New York University and Manhattan College. Two years later, John R. Flannery, sometimes called "the father of American lacrosse," helped form the United States National Amateur Lacrosse Association (USNALA). In 1883, the Intercollegiate Lacrosse Association followed, and members included Harvard, Yale, Princeton, New York University, Lehigh, and Stevens Institute. All of these schools still have field lacrosse teams today. Affluent Americans particularly fancied lacrosse, which they viewed as a gentlemen's game. Though "flesh-and-blood Iroquois Indians had played an important role in the early years ... American organizers reserved a very marginal place for native peoples."[14] The game flourished in the Northeast, particularly in New York. Soon, Maryland became a hotbed of lacrosse activity, as affluent, established families in Baltimore adopted the game. For example, "six grandnephews of author [and Baltimore celebrity] Edgar Allan Poe built up the game at Princeton [University]."[15] The Baltimore college that most exemplified this trend was Johns Hopkins, which began introducing lacrosse in various forms in the mid-1880s. To this day, Johns Hopkins remains a powerhouse in men's lacrosse, competing almost yearly for collegiate titles with other eastern U.S. universities. Additionally, some of the more important books on lacrosse and its history have been written by those affiliated with Johns Hopkins.

### Fast Break!

There are three hotbeds of lacrosse in the United States: Maryland, Upstate New York, and Long Island, New York.

## Lacrosse Across the Pond

In the 19th century, lacrosse spread to the British Isles. Given the sport's popularity in Canada, it was a natural progression that lacrosse would garner interest in the mother country. Teams sprang up in London, Manchester, and Liverpool, which are all in England, and even in Belfast in Northern Ireland. In particular, Manchester became a hotbed of the sport to rival Maryland, New York, and eastern Canada. In 1883, the sport received a boost in England when the Canadian dentist, Dr. Beers, brought a team comprised of Native American and white players across the Atlantic Ocean. They played 48 exhibitions in England and a dozen more in Scotland and Ireland. The games drew large crowds that on one occasion, included the Prince of Wales. In 1884, a British writer wrote in the *Saturday Review of London* that in order to master lacrosse, a player needed "the feet of [Greek warrior] Achilles, the hands of [another fearsome Greek warrior] Diomedes, and the craft of [the wiliest of Greek warriors] Odysseus."[16]

Lacrosse was included among the sports at the 1908 Summer Olympic Games in London, England (It had also been played at the 1904 Olympics in St. Louis, Missouri.), though only Canada and the United Kingdom sent teams. Canada, the strongest team, won the gold medal as expected.

*Manchester, England, discovered lacrosse in the 19th century and remains a center of lacrosse to this day. An early 1900s lacrosse game in Manchester is shown here.*

## Early 20th-Century Lacrosse

The sport continued to grow in the new century, as American college campuses remained the hub of lacrosse life. The United States Intercollegiate Lacrosse League (USILL) was founded in 1905 and included a northern and southern division, though teams were still concentrated in the eastern part of the country. The game's continued growth lessened for a few years during World War I, but when the war ended, the popularity of lacrosse began to surge once more.

The early 20th century saw the creation of new rules that would forever change the men's game. In 1921, an offside rule dictated that only midfielders could run the entire field. Defensive and offensive players were prohibited from crossing the center line. This prevented teams from massing defensive players in front of their goal to prevent the other team from scoring.

## *The Lacrosse Field*

The 10 players per men's team compete on a rectangular field that measures 110 yards (100.6 m) long by 60 yards (55 m) wide. By comparison, the women's field, on which 12 players compete, is 120 yards (109.7 m) long by 70 yards (64 m) wide. Until 2006, the women's field did not have an out-of-bounds area, and women were allowed to chase an errant ball outside the lines. Now, women must abide by a strict solid line boundary.

The fields are divided in half by a midfield line, with an "X" at the center where face-offs (for men) and draw controls (for women) occur. There are also restraining lines at 30 yards (27 m) from each end line for women and 35 yards (32 m) for men, which signal the area of confinement for offensive and defensive players. Around each goal is the crease—a circle with a 9-foot (2.7 m) radius into which offensive players may not step. Players were formerly able to jump into the crease and, if they put the ball in the goal before landing, it would count. The National Collegiate Athletic Association (NCAA) outlawed the so-called "crease dive" in the late 1980s after Gary Gait's famous "Air Gait" dive, but it is still legal in professional and international play.

Like ice hockey, lacrosse is a sport where the area behind the goal is in play. Offensive players routinely move behind the goal to set up passes and shots. The goal—a 6-foot (1.8 m) square—sits 15 yards (13.7 m) from the end line.

The ample size of the lacrosse field ensures a wide-open, quick-moving game that demonstrates the unique abilities of its athletes.

## Fast Break!

Lacrosse is now played in more than 20 countries on 5 continents: Australia, Asia, North America, South America, and Europe.

In 1933, additional new rules were enacted. In an effort to speed up play and make the game more exciting, the number of players was reduced from 12 to 10, and the length of the playing field shrank from 110 yards (100.6 m) to 80 yards (73 m), although it was later changed back to 110 yards. The playing area at the rear of each goal was set at 20 yards (18.3 m). The modern lacrosse team now consisted of three attackmen, three midfielders, three defensemen, and one goalie.

## The Rise of Intercollegiate Lacrosse

Well into the mid-20th century, lacrosse was still a regional game. The United States Intercollegiate Lacrosse League (USILL) was replaced in 1926 by the United States Intercollegiate Lacrosse Association (USILA). USILA oversaw men's lacrosse championships until 1971, when the NCAA began to hold men's lacrosse playoffs. Maryland dominated college lacrosse from the 1920s to the 1970s, with Johns Hopkins, Navy, University of Maryland, and St. John's leading the way. The first NCAA champion, however, was Cornell University in Ithaca, New York, as the center of power in men's lacrosse spread north.

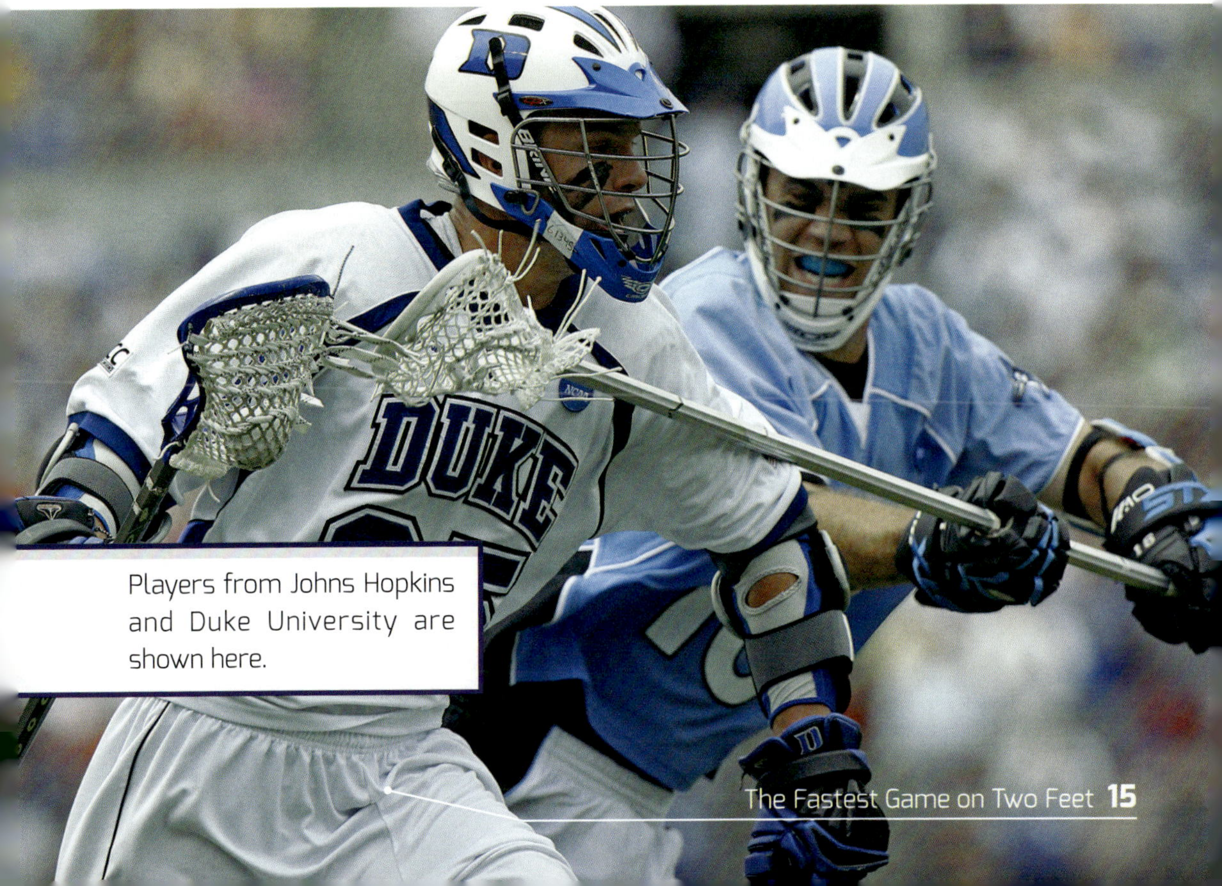


Players from Johns Hopkins and Duke University are shown here.

*Men's*

# LACROSSE FIELD

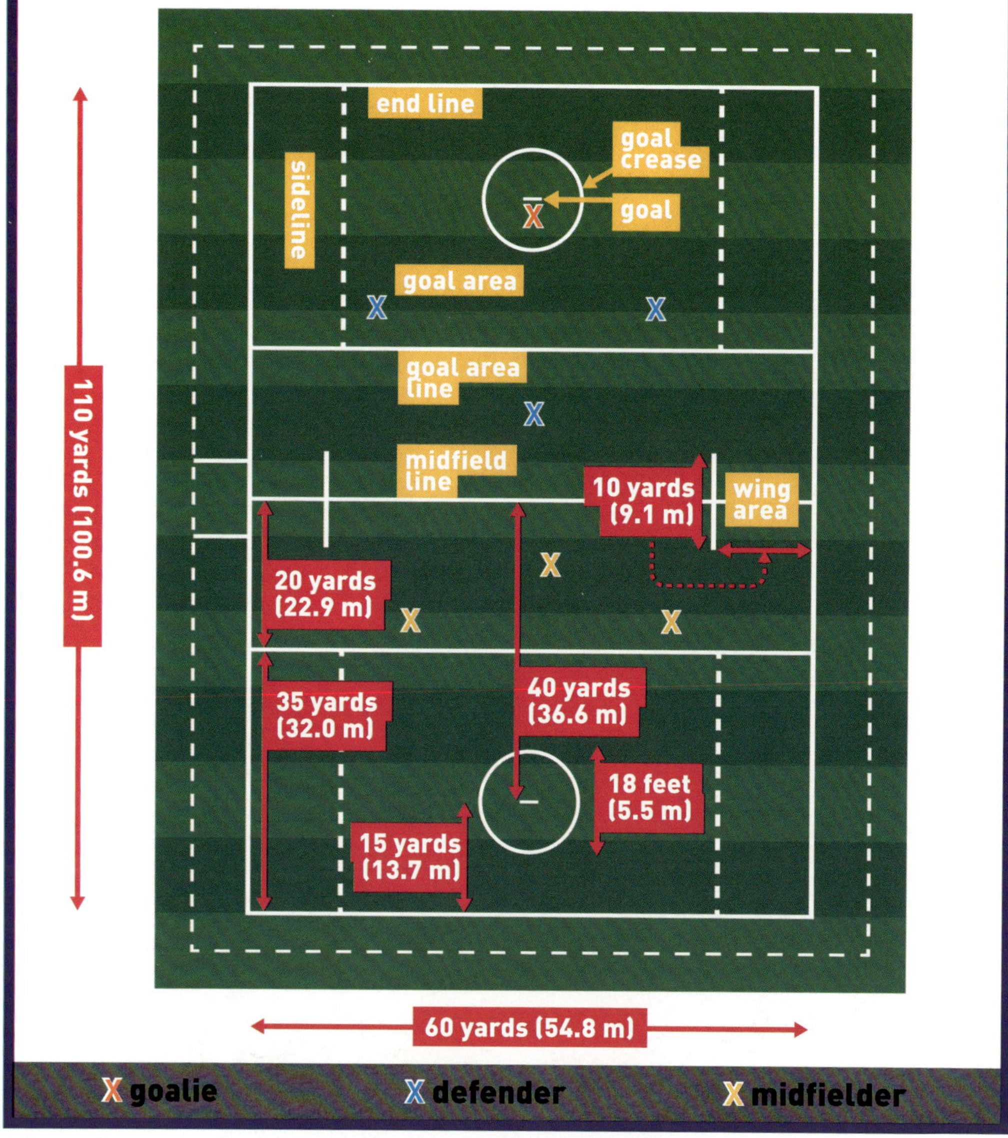


*These diagrams show the dimensions and player positions on men's and women's lacrosse fields. Because women's lacrosse is different from men's, there are substantial differences between the two fields and the player alignments.*

*Women's*
# LACROSSE FIELD

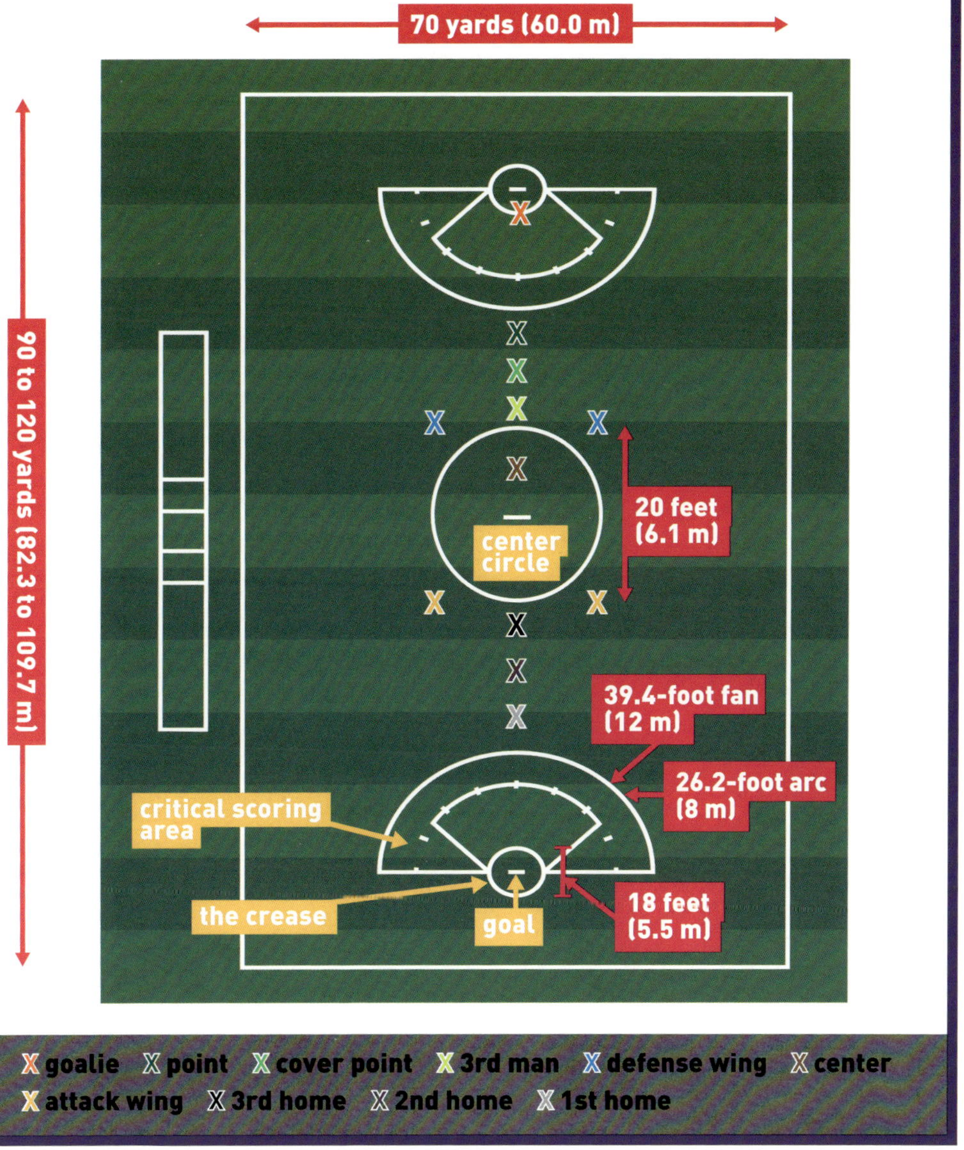

One of the greatest players to ever don lacrosse gear is better known for playing another sport. Jim Brown, who grew up playing football and lacrosse on Long Island, became famous at Syracuse University in the 1950s as an All-American running back, and later as a fullback in the National Football League (NFL) for the Cleveland Browns. A lesser-known fact is that while at Syracuse, Brown established a reputation as a great lacrosse midfielder; his combination of size, strength, and speed made him an ideal lacrosse player.

Syracuse University dominated the NCAA tournaments for years, winning 11 championships between 1983 and 2009. (One of these was vacated, however, due to rules violations.) Also winning championships was the usual cast of lacrosse powers: Johns Hopkins, Maryland, Princeton, Cornell, University of North Carolina at Chapel Hill, Duke, and University of Virginia. In 2015, University of Denver crashed the eastern U.S. lacrosse party, winning its first national lacrosse championship and threatening to make the game a

## Lacrosse Comes to the Simpsons

Lacrosse came to network television in November 2016 as *The Simpsons* made the sport a central focus in the episode entitled "There Will Be Buds." In the 28th season of the animated series, Homer Simpson and his friend Kirk Van Houten sign their kids up to play the sport as an alternative to football. Matt Selman, the show's executive producer, worked hard to satisfy lacrosse fans by making the episode as authentic as possible. Lisa Simpson and the rest of the lacrosse-playing children were even shown a video of the Gait brothers playing at Syracuse University.

Gary Gait, an admitted Simpson's fan, was clearly flattered by the appearance: "I was joking around saying, 'What else is there to do now?' ... 'I made it on *The Simpsons.*' I can retire and get out of lacrosse. It's over. ... It was fun. I never would have thought it was going to happen."[1]

Neither Selman nor any of his crew had ever played lacrosse, but they worked hard to please lacrosse aficionados. They watched lacrosse games on the Internet, read a lacrosse dictionary, and checked the script with former lacrosse players. "'It was really fun to dig into that world and delve into it,' Selman said. 'I hope [lacrosse fans] were happy with the show.'"[2]

1. Quoted in Matt Hamilton, "Lacrosse Gets the Simpson's Treatment." Munday Lacrosse, November 9, 2016. www.mundaylacrosse.com/news_article/show/719806?referrer_id=2914595.
2. Hamilton, "Lacrosse Gets the Simpson's Treatment."

national one. They were the first-ever team outside of the eastern time zone to win the NCAA lacrosse tournament.

## Professional Lacrosse

Unlike basketball, baseball, or football, lacrosse for many years had no professional league to which the best college players might aspire. Instead, such players typically joined amateur club teams. In 1987, the Major Indoor Lacrosse League (MILL) played its first season. In 2001, Major League Lacrosse (MLL) became the first outdoor field lacrosse organization. Founding franchises in the MLL included teams in Boston, Massachusetts; Bridgeport, Connecticut; Long Island, New York; Baltimore, Maryland; New Jersey; and Rochester, New York.

The league has both gained and lost teams during its short history, as it struggled to gain a foothold among the more popular American spectator sports. As of 2017, there were nine franchises, including the Denver Outlaws and the Atlanta Blaze, playing a summer schedule. The Long

*John Grant Jr. (#24) is regarded as one of the all-time lacrosse greats.*

Island Lizards won the first championship in 2001, and the Denver Outlaws claimed the league title in 2016. Average attendance for league games is between 4,000 and 6,000, which trails far behind attendance at other major sporting events in the United States. Low box office figures played a part in the folding of several franchises, including those in the California cities of Los Angeles and San Francisco. Even so, the MLL continues to eye expansion and has attracted some of the best men's lacrosse players in the world, including brothers Gary and Paul Gait; John Grant Jr.; Paul Rabil; brothers Casey, Ryan, and Mike Powell; and Rob Pannell.

## Women's Lacrosse

The first women's lacrosse game was played in Scotland in 1890. The first U.S. game did not take place until 1926 in the friendly confines of Baltimore, Maryland. Despite the late start, the women's game has grown tremendously, particularly since the NCAA began including women's lacrosse in 1982. Women's lacrosse varies greatly from the men's game; the main difference is the amount of contact the players are allowed. Women's rules prohibit the body checking that characterizes the men's game, and, as a result, female players do not wear the same protective garb, including helmets and padding, that

Hilary Bowen (# 1) and Hannah Nielsen (# 7) helped lead Northwestern's women's lacrosse team to multiple NCAA titles.

one sees on male players. The women's game, therefore, relies more on finesse than on toughness.

As with men's intercollegiate lacrosse, teams from the eastern time zone have dominated women's play. Maryland has won the NCAA title a dozen times, with Princeton, Virginia, North Carolina, Penn State, and Temple all claiming multiple championships. However, one midwestern team has also found great success among this group: Northwestern. The team from Chicago was dominant between 2005 and 2012, claiming seven titles.

## Continued Growth

In the 21st century, lacrosse has continued to expand. It is among the fastest growing sports in the United States at all levels—youth, high school, and college—and is quickly moving from an east-coast phenomenon to a nationwide activity. Girls' lacrosse is showing explosive growth at all levels. The sport has struggled to gain traction out west, yet recent figures show that many more California schools have started lacrosse programs. With its popularity rising continuously, lacrosse seems to have a bright future within the American sports scene.

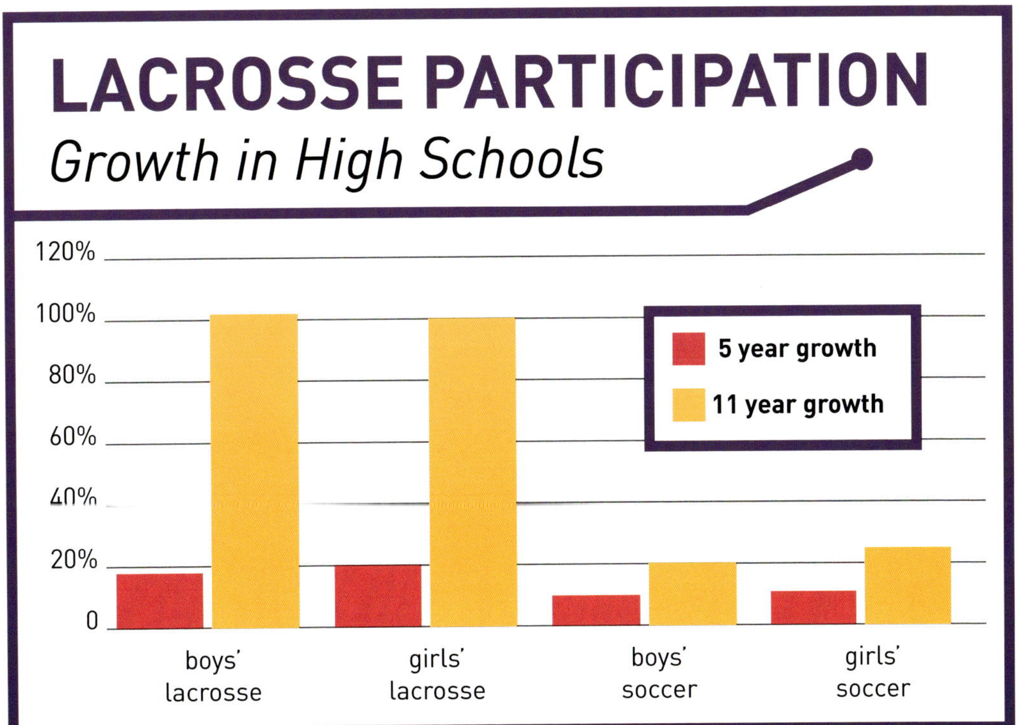


*Lacrosse has experienced explosive growth in the 21st century, as this data from the National Federation of State High School Associations shows.*

Chapter 2

# The Biomechanics of Lacrosse

The three main items needed to play the game of lacrosse are the lacrosse stick, the ball, and the goal. Various aspects of a player's equipment and how they use that equipment can affect their success on the field. The science behind how these items are used and how players should maneuver their bodies gives players useful knowledge on how to improve their own lacrosse skills.

This chapter delves into the science behind shooting a lacrosse ball, a goaltender's reaction time, and the art of the face-off. Each player's performance depends on their strength, agility, and precise timing of the movements required to play the sport.

## The Lacrosse Stick

"A stick, or crosse, is the lacrosse player's best friend,"[17] wrote journalist M. B. Roberts. Players are often exceedingly picky about their sticks; although the stick will not make a bad player into a good one, a good stick is a vital tool of the trade. According to US Lacrosse, the men's lacrosse stick must be an overall length of 40 to 42 inches (102 to 107 cm) for attackmen and midfielders; 52 to 72 inches (132 to 183 cm) for defensemen; and 40 to 72 inches (102 to 183 cm) for goalies. Shorter sticks allow for more agility and better shooting. Longer sticks allow defensemen to stick check the offensive players from a greater distance.

For younger players, these rules are waived. Young lacrosse players are encouraged to use sticks from 30 to 40 inches (76 to 102 cm) to enable them to control the stick more adeptly.

*These traditional wooden lacrosse sticks and balls were used by Native Americans many years ago.*

## Fast Break!

It is fun to practice lacrosse with a partner, but it can be practiced without a partner, too, as long as there is a wall.

The head of a lacrosse stick must be 6.5 to 10 inches (16.5 to 25.4 cm) wide, except for the goalie's stick, which is 10 to 12 inches (25.4 to 30.5 cm) across. This wider head enables the goalie to stop more shots. The depth of the pocket of a men's lacrosse stick is also strictly governed. (Women's sticks have much shallower pockets.) A pocket is illegal if the "top surface of a lacrosse ball, when placed in the head of the crosse [stick], is below the bottom edge of the side wall."[18]

Beginner players are also encouraged to use a mesh pocket instead of a strung pocket. The soft mesh pocket "makes catching and throwing easier and helps with overall skill development."[19]

## Lacrosse Stick Technology

In the 21st century, the traditional lacrosse stick appears as foreign and ancient as the first cell phones do to smartphone users. Originally made of wood, leather, and animal byproducts such as deer sinew, lacrosse sticks now feature state-of-the-art components. Sticks that used to look like a giant spoon are now sleek technological marvels with light, strong shafts and a variety of head shapes and sizes designed for maximum effectiveness on the field.

A major development in stick technology was the creation of an offset head. Bill Brine developed this type of lacrosse stick, in which the pocket is shifted down from the plane of the stick, after he noticed that the Gait brothers were using slightly bent shafts for a better tactile response. An offset head made the ball sit lower in the pocket and gave the player a heightened sense of control. Players had a better feel for the ball in the pocket. Pretty soon, almost all players were using the first stick that employed this technology, the Brine Edge. Stick shaft materials have also evolved. Today's shafts may be made of materials such as aluminum, titanium, scandium, carbon fiber composites, and various alloys.

Offset heads, combined with mesh pockets and plastic frames, have changed the game of lacrosse. A beginner player can buy a stick right off the store rack and immediately feel a sense of control that players of old could not. This development has helped grow the game of lacrosse.

For centuries, the lacrosse stick was fashioned from hickory wood and leather. That changed dramatically in the mid-20th century with the introduction of light metals and plastic. As journalist John McPhee wrote, "The event is sometimes called the plasticization of lacrosse. It changed the game to the same great extent that pole-vaulting was changed when fibreglass replaced bamboo."[20] These innovations in stick technology have resulted in numerous benefits: Sticks are less expensive, sturdier, easier to match to individual player's needs, lighter, easier to handle, and more durable. Players have been using this technology since the 1970s, though some players continued to use wooden sticks. However, almost all lacrosse players "now play with synthetic sticks, usually made of a titanium shaft and a plastic head."[21] The heads are generally molded from a plastic called Surlyn (manufactured by DuPont) that is strong enough to withstand the punishment of a typical lacrosse game. Players commonly customize their sticks, and the shaft and head are often chosen individually. As McPhee wrote, "Ask a modern player what he has in his hands, and, typically, he might say, 'Cyber head on a black Swizzle Scandium.' Next player: 'A Penitrator head on a Gait Anarchy shaft.' Next: 'An Evolution 2.0 on a Kryptolyte shaft.'"[22]

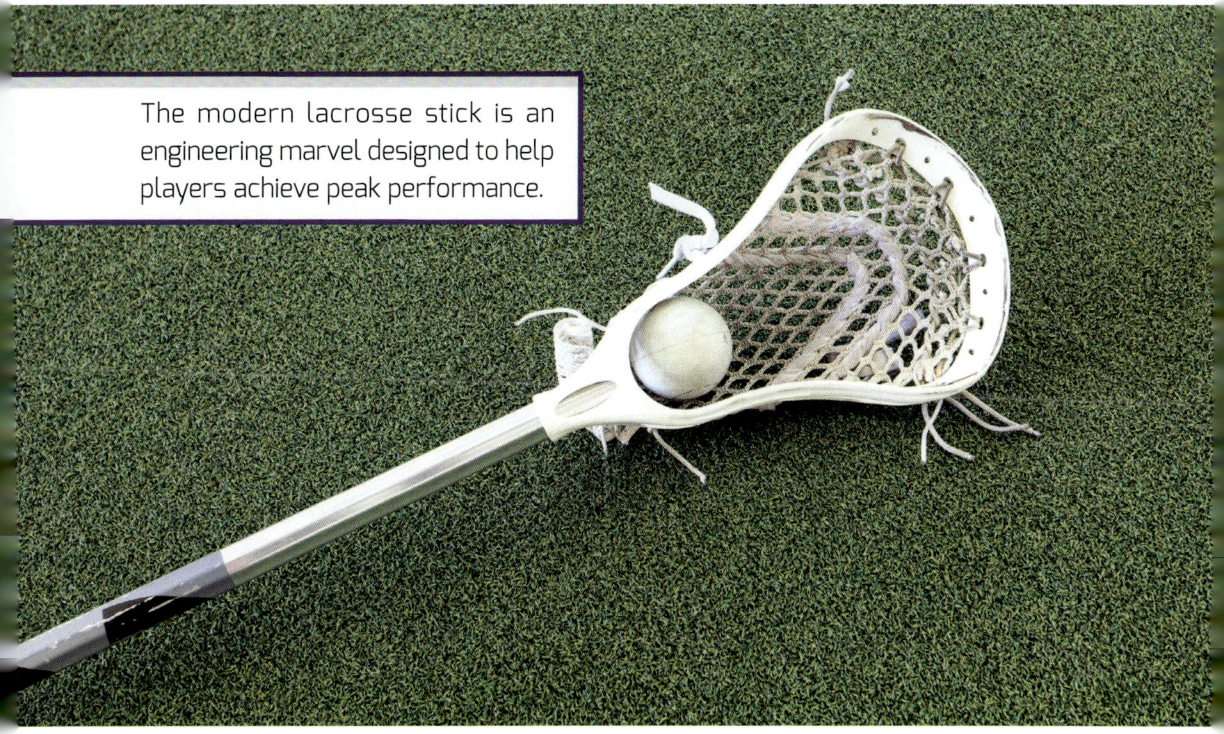

The modern lacrosse stick is an engineering marvel designed to help players achieve peak performance.

## The Ball

The lacrosse ball, often referred to as the "Indian rubber ball," is an ordinary looking projectile about the size of a tennis ball. A tennis ball is only 2.1 ounces (59.5 g), whereas a lacrosse ball is 5 to 5.5 ounces (141.7 to 156 g). It is solid and much harder than a tennis ball and in the professional game, can be whipped from the pocket of the lacrosse stick at dizzying speeds of more than 100 miles (161 km) per hour. Orange, yellow, and lime green balls are allowable, but the lacrosse ball is most commonly white.

There are strict rules regarding the bounce of the solid rubber lacrosse ball. US Lacrosse dictates that regulation balls, when dropped from a height of 6 feet (1.8 m), must bounce between a minimum of 43 inches (109.2 cm) and a maximum of 51 inches (129.5 cm). The maximum height represents a 70 percent rebound from the starting height. This test must be conducted on a concrete floor at a set temperature.

The amount a ball bounces compared to the height from which it is dropped is referred to as the "rebound ratio" or "rebound rating." This ratio can be figured by dividing the length of the rebound by the length of the drop. Since a regulation lacrosse ball must bounce between 43 and 51 inches (109.2 and 129.5 cm), its rebound ratio is between 59.7 and 70.8 percent. By comparison, a tennis ball has a rebound ratio of between 53 and 58 percent when dropped on the same type of concrete floor. Golf balls have a relatively high rebound ratio, while baseballs are not known for bouncing well and have a lower rebound ratio.

The relatively "bouncy" quality of the lacrosse ball can be of significance when an offensive player shoots at the goal. These shots can be difficult for a goalie to stop due to the unpredictability of how high and how true the ball will bounce off an uneven surface such as grass. The high rebound ratio can also be useful when players train using the so-called "wall ball" method (repeatedly throwing the ball against a concrete wall and catching it).

## The Goal

The focus of every team is the goal area and trying to get the lacrosse ball into the net. The goal itself consists of two vertical poles 6 feet (1.8 m) high, with one horizontal 6-foot (1.8 m) pole separating the two. The back of the goal contains netting that must prevent rebounds from occurring. This 6-foot-by-6-foot (1.8 m by 1.8 m) square is surrounded on all sides by the "crease," a circle with a diameter of 18 feet (5.5 m), into which offensive players cannot step. If an offensive player scores while entering the crease, the goal is nullified.

The goalie, who is outfitted with extra padding and protection and a

*Gary Gait's (#22) crease dive was so innovative that it completely surprised the opposing team.*

stick with a wider net, must protect this 6-foot (1.8 m) square area. This requires quickness, agility, and instincts. Unlike soccer and hockey teams, which rarely see high-scoring games, a lacrosse team can often score between 10 and 20 or more goals in a game. Thus, as David G. Pietramala wrote, "The goalie's position is probably the most important on the field."[23] With shots hurtling at them, the goalie's quick movements and stick skills may be all that separates their team from being on the wrong side of a score.

The goalie's job is to guard a 6-foot-by-6 foot (1.8 m by 1.8 m) goal.

## Air Gait

Arguably, the most famous lacrosse shot in NCAA lacrosse history was first performed by Gary Gait of Syracuse University in 1988. The move, also called the crease dive, is now banned in NCAA play.

In lacrosse, a player may not enter the area around the goal—the crease—unless the ball is already in the net. Any goal scored by a player whose foot is even on the crease line will be overturned.

In the NCAA Division I playoffs in 1988, Syracuse faced off with the University of Pennsylvania in the semifinals. With his team trailing 2–1, Gait scored in a manner that no one had ever seen before. From behind the net, his feet outside the crease, he leaped like a basketball player attempting a dunk, and before landing, stuffed the ball into the net over a shocked University of Pennsylvania goaltender. He scored once more on the same move in the third quarter to tie the game at 4. The officials allowed the goal, as there was no rule about the crease extending upward. As per the rules, Gait did not land in the crease until the ball was in the net.

Thanks in part to Gary Gait's now famous maneuver, Syracuse University went on to win the NCAA national championship that year.

## The Biomechanics of the Lacrosse Shot

Lacrosse has famously been called "the fastest game on two feet,"[24] so it is not surprising that velocity, momentum, force, and acceleration all factor into the sport. While the players are often seen sprinting from one end to the other, weaving or dodging among defenders or checking each other with powerful blows, there is one thing on the field that moves at a far greater speed: the lacrosse ball.

Paul Rabil, former Johns Hopkins University star and multiple MLL MVP, first recorded the fastest shot of a lacrosse ball: 111 miles (178.6 km) per hour. According to ESPN's Sport Science feature on Rabil, a 105-mile (169 km) per hour shot from 60 feet (18.3 m) away reaches the goal in 0.39 second. From a distance of 30 feet (9.1 m), that time is reduced to "under nineteen-hundredths of a second."[25] As John McPhee wrote, "A lacrosse stick is a rigid slingshot."[26]

### Fast Break!

Kyle Hartzell now shares the record with Paul Rabil for the fastest lacrosse shot at 111 miles (178.6 km) per hour.

*Paul Rabil, shown here, has clocked the fastest lacrosse shot of all time.*

According to ESPN Sport Science host, John Brenkus, "The secret to Rabil's blazing shot is a combination of biomechanics and physics."[27] The farther the ball is from the axis of rotation (the center of the torso), the quicker its linear momentum. "Linear momentum (p) is the product of mass (m) and velocity (v); the momentum of the player … created by his weight and speed as he approaches the goal (p = mv), turns the static lacrosse ball into an unstoppable projectile."[28] When a player such as Rabil takes a shot, their arm and the 40-inch (102 cm) stick act as a series of levers, "extending the ball as far as 62 inches (158 cm) from the main axis of rotation"[29] and propelling the ball forward. As the player drives their foot into the turf, the friction that is created "is where linear momentum begins its conversion to rotational momentum, as the shooter transfers energy from his planted foot through his legs and hips, up the torso and into his shoulders."[30]

## Fast Break!

In order to beat a defender and take a shot at the opposing team's goal, every offensive player practices the skill of dodging. Dodging enables a player to run past the defense toward the goal.

Superior biomechanics allows Rabil to maximize the speed of his shot. As he drives his foot into the ground, friction against the turf allows him to convert his forward momentum into rotational momentum as his body revolves toward the goal. His shoulders rotate 1,350 degrees per second as he unleashes the shot.

Rabil himself explains that a lacrosse shot should be executed with the power of a football middle linebacker hitting another player or a heavyweight boxer punching an opponent. If a player working on shooting drills is not breathing heavily after five to ten shots, there is something lacking in the player's effort, Rabil believes. "Anchor your legs, kick them out, follow through, use your hips, tighten up your core, rotate your core, turn your elbow, release your elbow, follow all the way through to your shot … and that's tiring,"[31] he said.

## The Science of Goaltending

Given the velocity of the lacrosse shot, the instincts, reaction time, and agility of the goalie are of paramount importance in preventing opposing goals. At 36 square feet (3.3 sq m), the field lacrosse goal is 50 percent larger than its counterpart in ice hockey.

According to ESPN Sport Science, "All else being equal, a lacrosse goalie creates an obstacle about 17% smaller than a hockey goalie."[32] The Sport Science study argues that "some lacrosse shots are literally impossible to defend because of the physical limits of the human body."[33] The fastest a human can react to visual stimuli is roughly

0.20 second. However, as seen in the discussion of the speed of the lacrosse shot, at 105 miles (169 km) per hour from 30 feet (9.1 m), the ball will reach the net in 0.19 second, which makes it virtually impossible for the goalie to react. To demonstrate the goalie's reactions, Sport Science used Penn State alumnus and MLL star goalie Drew Adams. About one-third of a second before a shot is released, Adams's eyes focus on the stick's head, trying to judge the shot's location. He typically begins moving for the save just 0.12 second after the ball is released by the attacking player. To make a play, Adams extends his stick at a rate of 0 to 20 miles (0 to 32.2 km) per hour in just 0.125 second, an acceleration "on par with a rattlesnake strike."[34] Brenkus called the goalie position "possibly the most unfair position in sports" because the average save percentage in NCAA lacrosse was only 51 percent, or, as he says, "basically a coin toss."[35]

*New York Lizards goalie Drew Adams is shown here guarding the net against the Denver Outlaws.*

## The Science of the Face-Off

The face-off, which takes place at the beginning of each period and after each goal, may be the most important play in lacrosse. According to Alan McLiverty, a Rochester chapter US Lacrosse president, "a good faceoff guy and a hot goalie"[36] alone can be the difference between winning and losing. So important are the players who participate in the face-off that there are often face-off specialists who only square off at the X in the center of the field for this important play. Known as FOGOs (Face-off Get-off), these players will sprint off the field as soon as one team gains possession. Then, they will wait their turn for the all-important next face-off.

The face-off specialist combines confidence, technique, effort, agility, and strength. Coaches will sometimes look at veterans of wrestling to fill the face-off position, as success in these two endeavors is a result of many of the same characteristics, particularly agility and quickness. According to star FOGO Greg Gurenlian, whose win percentage in the MLL generally tops .600, "natural hand speed [and] nervous system reaction"[37] are key ingredients.While the average person reacts to auditory stimuli in about 0.15 second, Gurenlian only takes 0.13 second to begin moving his stick toward the ball. This gives him a 13 percent advantage over the average person. Using a double-over motorcycle grip (the way a motorcyclist grabs

## Biomechanics Defined

A midfielder or attackman sprints toward the goal, dodging defensive players. They push off their left foot, rise up, and twist their torso, launching a blistering shot toward the goal. In doing so, they alter the motion of their body. During the push off, they redirect their motion from horizontal to the rotational motion required to launch the shot. This is the type of motion that is considered in biomechanical analysis.

Biomechanics is the science of physical principles applied to biological systems, in this case, the human body. One area of biomechanics is kinematics, which describes the temporal (time) and spatial (distance) components of movement. The study of forces that act on the body is called kinetics. Forces such as gravity and contact with other objects (such as the foot pushing off the ground) cause the motion of the human body to change. The study of the way forces cause the body to move is called kinematic analysis.

the handlebar, making two overhand fists), Gurenlian swings his left hand (which is farther down the stick; the right hand is near the head) at 770 degrees per second, clamping on to the ball in 0.15 second, which allows him "to beat his opponent by just two-hundredths of a second."[38] During the 2015 season, Gurenlian used this ability and technique to record a face-off win percentage of 73 percent, a stunning win percentage in the competitive world of FOGOs. It is no surprise that his team, the New York Lizards, won the MLL championship that year.

*Face-off specialist Greg Gurenlian (right) has exceptional hand speed and reaction time.*

Chapter 3

# Training for Endurance, Agility, and Strength

Lacrosse is a sport that demands fitness. At any time, midfielders sprint from one end to the other. Because male lacrosse players can hit each other with almost reckless abandon, the players wear protective gear; boys' lacrosse equipment generally includes a helmet, elbow pads, rib pads, shoulder pads, gloves, an athletic supporter and cup. Carrying this extra weight around a field containing more square feet than a football field is strenuous, and a well-trained body is pretty much mandatory. Offensive and defensive players and goalies do not have to run the distances that midfielders must, but they tend to stay on the field longer than the rotating midfielders. Still, endurance training for midfielders is a must, and their aerobic endurance often compares favorably with traditional distance athletes.

Lacrosse is not as popular or as widely played as the major American sports of football, hockey, basketball, baseball, or even soccer, and its surge in popularity is fairly recent. Consequently, fewer studies have been carried out on lacrosse athletes, and there is not as much scientific information available when it comes to training as there is for more popular sports. Nevertheless, it is clear that successful lacrosse athletes must have a combination of endurance, size, strength, power, speed, and agility.

*Boys' lacrosse requires a lot of equipment.*

## Fast Break!

NFL players who formerly played lacrosse include wide receiver Chris Hogan, placekicker Steven Hauschka, and the late Baltimore Colts tight end and hall of famer John Mackey.

## Training for Endurance: The Lactic Acid Debate

Almost all team sports involve running, some more than others. Lacrosse, like soccer or basketball, is a sport of continual movement. While offensive and defensive players are limited in their movements on the field, midfielders have no such boundaries. Even so, all

*Lacrosse players are almost always running. Endurance training is a must.*

players must be in top physical shape to compete effectively, and the type of endurance that lacrosse demands is often best addressed in the off-season.

A combination of long-distance running and sprinting can be effective for lacrosse players. Speed is an ingrained trait, and though players can increase their speed through training, if they are not born with the right genes, no amount of training will turn them into a sprinter. Endurance, on the other hand, can be increased dramatically, though here too, unless players are born with certain physical gifts, they will never be Olympic marathoners.

When athletes talk about barriers to peak performance, the topic often turns to lactic acid buildup. The traditional theory about lactic acid goes like this: When athletes engage in strenuous exercise, the body directs additional oxygen to its muscles. This energy normally comes from glucose, a sugar that is the human body's key source of energy. The body breaks this sugar down into a substance called pyruvate, which is further broken down to supply the body with energy during sporting activities. This is the human body's preferred method for generating energy. However, when the going really gets tough and oxygen runs low, the body turns from aerobic (oxygenated) fuel to anaerobic fuel. Anaerobic energy occurs when the body converts pyruvate into lactate, which enables the breakdown of glucose to continue, producing additional energy without needing oxygen. However, high lactate levels increase the acidity of muscle cells and disrupt the metabolic system. Energy breakdown cannot function well in an acidic environment, and the athlete begins to feel fatigue, that "hitting the wall" sensation that so many athletes complain of when they run out of energy.

According to conventional scientific wisdom, lactic acid actually serves a useful purpose. It is the body's way of telling athletes that they are excessively exerting themselves. This prevents permanent damage to the athlete as a result of pushing too hard. The production of lactate in the body leads to a burning sensation in the muscles, which alerts athletes to cease overworking the body.

For many years, it was believed that muscle soreness was a result of lactic acid buildup. This traditional belief has been challenged. Instead, most research now indicates that the dull pain athletes often feel 24 to 72 hours after an intense workout, called Delayed Onset Muscle Soreness (DOMS), is most likely a result of "actual muscle cell damage and an elevated release of various metabolites into the tissue surrounding the muscle cells."[39] When researchers measured lactic acid levels following exercise, they found no significant correlation with the amount of muscle soreness felt in the aftermath of intense physical activity. Instead, scientists observed that certain types of physical activity trigger DOMS. One such example occurs in what is called eccentric muscle contractions. An eccentric contraction happens "when a muscle lengthens against a load—imagine your flexed arms attempting to catch a thousand pound weight."[40] Activities that require many eccentric contractions, such as running downhill, result in the most severe soreness a day or so later. Lactic acid buildup is not necessarily the culprit.

Recently, researchers such as George A. Brooks, professor of integrative biology at the University of California, Berkeley, have challenged the traditional notions about lactic acid. Brooks believes that rather than being the athlete's enemy, it is instead fuel for the muscles. In experiments with laboratory rats, Brooks found that the rats "burned [lactic acid] faster than anything else I could give them."[41] Subsequent experiments with humans produced similar results.

As Gina Kolata wrote, "The understanding now is that muscle cells convert glucose or glycogen to lactic acid. The lactic acid is taken up and used as a fuel by mitochondria, the energy factories in muscle cells."[42] Interestingly, Brooks observes, coaches have been ahead of scientists in designing training for endurance. They have recognized that performance improved when athletes worked on endurance by running longer distances. This type of training "increased the mass of their muscle mitochondria, letting them burn more lactic acid and allowing the muscles to work harder and longer."[43] Having athletes work out strenuously in brief spurts was also found to be beneficial: placing this type of stress on the muscles increases mitochondria mass, according to Brooks.

## Body Checking

As in ice hockey, checking an opponent with the stick or the body is allowed in men's lacrosse. (In women's lacrosse, stick checking is only allowed.) Body checking, the act of hitting a player on the other team—even to the extent of knocking the player off his feet, is viewed as a perfectly acceptable part of the game. Clean, hard checks in the open field are an added component of team play.

However, there are strict rules about which checks are allowed and which are not. A body check can only be performed against the ball carrier or a player within 5 yards (4.6 m) of a loose ball. It is illegal to body check below the knees, above the shoulders, or behind the back. Leading with the helmet will also draw a penalty. Body checking with the lacrosse stick is also illegal, so the stick should be held to the side when initiating a check.

A proper body check should be performed by making contact with the shoulders—similar to a shoulder block in football. Body checks most often occur when the opposing player attempts a shot, when trying to clear the crease on a loose ball in front of the goal, and when trying to gain an advantage during a loose ball. The best results of a body check are obtained when the player initiating contact keeps his head up and his feet under him for as long as possible. The arms should stay pinned against the body and both hands must remain on the stick. A controlled hit is always better than an overly aggressive one. The object, after all, is to gain possession of the ball, not to injure an opposing player.

Brooks believes that what separates great athletes from merely good athletes is the ability to produce and reuse more lactate. In a study comparing trained and untrained bicyclists, he found that "trained riders could produce and use about 60 percent more lactate."[44] While Brooks's studies suggest that slow, steady endurance training and high impact speed training both benefit athletes, one type of training, which most recreational athletes engage in, did not improve an athletes ability to produce and harness lactate. Writer Mark McClusky explained, "We'll go for a run or a bike ride at a tempo that feels … kinda hard. Certainly not easy, but not awful either. Unfortunately, that's probably the least beneficial workout for most of us—it would be better to either go really slow, building an aerobic base, or go really, really hard, working the anaerobic systems that provide our high-end power and speed."[45] While moderately hard workouts are obviously better than nothing, Brooks found, they do not maximize one's ability to produce and use lactate.

Again, Brooks's theories are just that, and many scientists and trainers disagree. More commonly, athletes are trained to be in good cardio (which means "heart") shape by doing just the opposite of Brooks's suggestions, working at 70 to 80 percent of the maximum heart rate. This will put them in the aerobic zone, the stage of a workout where the body uses stored oxygen. When athletes run at this pace, they improve the heart's ability to pump blood to the muscles, which also strengthens the respiratory system. This would involve working out at that "kinda hard" tempo that McClusky counsels against.

Given these competing theories, the best advice one can give about endurance and speed training is this: Ask a coach.

## Training for Strength, With and Without Weights

When it comes to training for lacrosse in the off-season, coaches generally recommend weight training right alongside running as a fundamental activity. The greatest lacrosse players tend to display a combination of speed and strength. When lacrosse fans discuss the greatest college players of all time, one name typically rises to the top: Jim Brown, the great NFL player who first played lacrosse at Syracuse University in the 1950s. In his senior year as a Syracuse midfielder, he scored an astounding total of 43 goals in a mere 10 games. Brown had a unique combination of size and strength. He stood 6 feet 2 inches (1.8 m) tall and weighed 230 pounds (104.3 kg). If he could not run by defenders (which he generally did), he would simply overpower them with his force. John Brenkus of ESPN's Sport Science calculated that Brown could produce "an estimated 1,000 pounds of force with each powerful stride," and that his shots were "generated with roughly 4,000 watts of peak power."[46]

*Jim Brown, the famous football player, is generally regarded as one of the all-time great athletes. Lacrosse was also a sport in which he had success.*

Though few players are in Brown's category, all top players must work on building up their arms, legs, and core through some form of strength training. A powerful body is especially important in a contact sport such as lacrosse, where aggressive body checking is routine. Mature athletes generally opt for weight training, but many physicians discourage younger athletes from using heavy weights until they are in high school. Players should always check with their doctors before beginning a weight-training regimen. However, even young players can benefit from strength training. Four common misconceptions about strength training for children are that it is not effective, that it impairs motor development, that it damages muscle and bone, and that it stunts growth. According to the *Encyclopedia of Sports Science*, edited by experts in medicine and physics from such universities as Michigan and Colorado, "None of the above notions is supported by research. A few studies do suggest that strength training before and during early puberty does not produce muscle hypertrophy [that is, build-up muscles], such training is still a good way to prevent injuries."[47] If young people do lift weights, guidelines include avoiding heavy loads. Weights should be light enough so that the young athlete can lift it 10 to 15 times. Also, "absolutely no maximum lifts"[48] are to be undertaken.

Fortunately, there are many other exercises young athletes can do to prepare for the rigorous nature of lacrosse. Calisthenics, which do not involve weights, include sit-ups and crunches to work the abdomen, push-ups for the chest and arms, lunges for the legs, and pull-ups to work the biceps and latissimus dorsi (back muscles below the arms). These exercises are effective at building up muscles and promoting endurance.

When a player is ready to begin off-season weight training, care should be taken to make sure that the exercises are right for the athlete. As M. B. Roberts wrote, "Every athlete is different, so it's best to consult with a trainer or your coach to create an individual plan, especially if you have not previously worked out with weights."[49] Roberts suggests working out with weights four days a week, working on the upper body two days and the lower for two days.

In *Women's Lacrosse: A Guide for Advanced Players and Coaches*, coach Janine Tucker and science writer Maryalice Yakutchik recommend three sessions a week on nonconsecutive days, such as Monday, Wednesday, and Friday. Standard exercises include the bench press, which works the chest, the triceps, and the deltoids (upper arms and shoulders); the military press, which works the triceps, deltoids, and trapezius (upper back); and biceps curls, which work the upper arms. Lower body training exercises, which include squats, dead lifts, leg extensions and curls, and the leg press, are common as well.

The human body contains more than 600 muscles, with the majority located above the waist. All muscles, wherever they are located, follow the physiological law of use and disuse. The more you use your muscles, the more they respond. Weight training acts on the muscles and the signals that nerves send to the muscles. Simplified, the process goes something like this: In order to exert force, the body signals motor units to contract. Motor units are nerves that connect to muscle fibers. Strength training improves the athlete's ability to call on motor units. This phenomenon is called muscle learning. This process increases strength even before the increase of muscle mass.

Muscles move the body and allow it to exert force because muscles, in turn, connect to tendons that move bones. When a muscle contracts, or shortens, it pulls on the tendon, which then causes the attached bone to move. Muscles are made up of muscle fibers, which are connected in bundles, and these muscle fibers are comprised of smaller units called myofibrils. Weight training causes the individual muscle fibers to grow by increasing the amount of myofibrils. Larger muscle fibers cause an athlete's muscles to grow bigger and stronger.

Weight training is associated with a wide range of benefits beyond lacrosse. Regular training can result in injury prevention, improved self-esteem, lifetime muscle and bone health, reduced risk of heart disease, improved body composition, and, some even believe, higher grades in school.

## Fast Break!

The top of the lacrosse stick is called the head or tip. The bottom of the pocket is called the throat.

## Training for Explosiveness: Plyometrics

Plyometrics, also known as "jump training" or "plyos," consists of exercises that originated in Europe. During these movements, muscles exert maximum force in short intervals of time, with the goal of increasing power. Such training is defined as "exercises that enable a muscle to reach maximum strength in as short a time as possible."[50] This training focuses on the athlete's learning to shift from a muscle extension to a contraction rapidly, or explosively. Plyometric drills were first used by Eastern Bloc athletes (athletes living in Communist states of Central and Eastern Europe) in the early 1970s. When athletes in track, weightlifting, and gymnastics began to show dramatic improvements, the rest of the world took notice.

Plyometric exercises are mostly associated with Olympic-style sports, but they are increasingly finding a place in lacrosse training, where developing "speed-strength ability … known as power"[51] is prized. As certified strength and conditioning specialist Billy J. Voltaire pointed out, "The term *power* in lay conversation is one that is often used interchangeably with strength. However, the two concepts are completely different, yet work in tandem."[52] According to Voltaire,

> *By definition, strength is the maximal amount of force generated in one effort. Power is calculated based on the amount*

*of force you can generate and how fast or explosive you are able to produce that force. The two work hand and hand. Without improving strength, it is difficult to improve your explosive abilities or be "powerful." Strength is usually measured by your 1RM (one-repetition max) and determines how strong you are.*[53]

Plyometric training focuses on developing the muscles. There are three types of muscle contractions: Eccentric contractions, which occur when the muscle lengthens under tension, are used in deceleration (slowing down); isometric contractions occur when the body comes to a stop; and concentric contractions result in acceleration. All three contractions commonly occur in every running stride, or when a lacrosse player plants their feet and then unleashes a shot. The period of isometric contraction, when the foot is on the ground, is also called the amortization phase. Plyometrics places an emphasis on getting off the ground as quickly as possible, limiting the time spent in this phase. An extended amortization phase results in wasted energy and loss of power. For this reason, many plyometric exercises involve hopping and jumping.

Plyometrics can build various types of power: starting power, accelerative power, and power endurance, for example. Each position on the lacrosse field has different demands, and specific plyometric training can be designed for midfielders, defensive players, offensive players, and goalies. As Voltaire explained,

*Starting power is simply the ability to explode from a resting or starting position, as done in a face-off, for example. Accelerative power is the ability to be continuously explosive with each stride as you sprint down field. Power endurance, as the name suggests, is the ability to maintain optimal power production over a long period of time while being resistant to fatigue.*[54]

Sample plyometric exercises recommended for lacrosse fitness include hopping on one foot, hopping in place with both feet, and jumping off a box placed on the ground and then jumping back up onto the box (termed a "depth jump"). As detailed in the book *Jumping into Plyometrics*, depth jumps from a box are done as follows:

*Equipment: A box 6 to 18 inches (15.2 to 45.7 cm) high*

*Start: Stand on the box with feet shoulder-width apart.*

*Action: Squat slightly and step from the box and drop to the floor. Attempt to quickly absorb the landing and "freeze" as soon as contact is made with the ground.*[55]

Plyometric exercises for the upper body often involve the use of a medicine ball, which is a large weighted

Plyometric drills often involve jumping repeatedly from one level to another.

ball. However, according to experts, "plyometric training is not recommended for prepubescent athletes because of the stress placed on the joints and its risk of premature closure of the growth plates."[56]

## Basic Training: Cradling the Ball

All lacrosse coaches and players agree that learning to cradle the lacrosse ball in the stick's pocket is central to mastering the sport of lacrosse. As longtime Georgetown lacrosse coach David Urick wrote, "Cradling is the rhythmical coordinated movement of the arms and wrists whose purpose is to stabilize the ball in the pocket of the stick."[57] Cradling is often the first skill that beginners are taught, and it takes significant practice time for a player to develop and master this skill.

In today's lacrosse, players must run up and down the field—often at top speed and through stick and body checks—while controlling the ball in the net of the stick. An effective cradle enables the player to run down the field at a high speed, all the while controlling the ball and keeping it ready for passing or shooting. When cradling, a player's top hand on the lacrosse stick does most of the work, while the bottom hand acts as a guide. David G. Pietramala explained that "the key to cradling is the looseness of the top hand's wrist. The loose wrist motion of the lacrosse player's top hand is comparable to a symphony conductor's handling of his baton."[58] When a conductor uses the baton, they move their arm and wrist, a motion similar to that which a lacrosse player uses to cradle. As players learn to cradle, they develop a "feel" for the weight of the ball in the stick. Learning to cradle is central to every other stick skill in the sport: catching, throwing, dodging, and shooting.

## Dodging

Every lacrosse player, whether playing offense or defense, has to learn the skill of dodging. Put simply, dodging is the act of shifting direction suddenly in order to avoid an opposition player. It is the equivalent of a basketball move, such as a crossover dribble, that confuses the opposition and enables the player to drive to the basket. Dodging allows an offensive player to outmaneuver a defensive player and have a clear shot at the goal. Dodging also allows a goalie to clear the ball with an opposing player in his face.

Dodgers need to be good at deception. They can fake one way and go another. They can change speeds. Some dodgers use a stutter-step to throw off the opponent. Common dodging techniques have names and are taught by coaches everywhere. They include the split dodge, face dodge, freeze dodge, bull dodge, and roll dodge. There are many more. Experienced players develop an arsenal of dodges in order to maneuver around the field more effectively.

Proper cradling technique creates what is often erroneously called a centrifugal force, which keeps the ball in the stick's netting. Centrifugal force has been defined as "the apparent force, equal and opposite to the centripetal force, drawing a rotating body away from the center of rotation, caused by the inertia of the body."[59] Thus the motion of the player's hands on the stick causes the lacrosse ball to rotate around the center of the netting. Centripetal force and centrifugal force are often confused. However, centripetal force is defined as a force that acts on a body moving in a circular path and is directed toward the center around which the body is moving. While centripetal force is real, centrifugal force does not actually exist. People feel it, and the ball moving in a circular motion behaves as if it is experiencing an outside force. However, it is not actually a real force.

Consider a ball attached to the end of a string. It can be swung over one's head, creating a circular motion. According to Isaac Newton's first law of motion, if the string was released, the ball would fly off in a straight line, as the force holding it in a circular pattern would be removed. However, when the string is still in one's hand, the ball experiences so-called centrifugal force, which keeps it circling around. The same is true of the lacrosse ball. Centrifugal force may not be a real force, but to the ball, it might as well be—the same way children on a merry-go-round do not experience any real outside force but still must exert their own force to keep from flying off the ride. Thus the player must keep the ball under control, exerting force on it, to keep it from flying out of the stick.

*Proper ball-cradling technique is essential if a player wants to keep the defender from dislodging it.*

Learning to cradle effectively, especially when running, dodging, or absorbing a check, takes hours of practice. In the women's game, cradling effectively can be even more difficult to master, because the netting in a women's lacrosse stick is shallower than in a men's lacrosse stick.

## Basic Training: The Physics of Wall Ball

When talking to lacrosse players about training, the subject of wall ball will invariably arise. "Playing wall ball from a young age improves your stick skills every day,"[60] said former collegiate player Scott Wilber. The exercise is simple: The player stands about 6 to 7 yards (5.5 to 6.4 m) from a smooth wall, preferably about 10 feet (3 m) high and as wide as possible. Using the lacrosse stick, the player hurls the lacrosse ball at the wall, catches the rebound, and repeats the process. Wall ball can be played when there is no one else to practice with, and nothing builds throwing and catching skills more quickly. As M.B. Roberts wrote, "Throwing against the wall gives players more opportunities to make contact with the ball—lax players call these 'touches'—than they'd get in a regular practice."[61] For this reason, wall ball is an excellent training exercise for the off-season.

The controlled environment of wall ball provides a good opportunity to investigate the physics of the lacrosse shot. All objects, the lacrosse ball included, are subject to the laws of motion set forth by famed English scientist Sir Isaac Newton in the late 17th century. Newton proposed three laws that describe moving bodies and provide the rules of physics that govern all lacrosse shots. These laws outline the relationship between any object, the forces that act upon it, and the resulting movement. They provided the basis for classical mechanics.

Newton's first law of motion states that an object in motion tends to stay in motion unless acted on by another force. The second law says that the acceleration of an object is related to the force acting upon it. The third law says that for every action, there is an equal and opposite reaction.

When a player throws the lacrosse ball against a wall, the wall and the ball exert force on each other as they make contact. The wall, of course, does not move, but the ball will ricochet off the wall. As Newton's first law indicates, the ball continues its original course until acted on by another force—in this case, the wall. Though the wall is not moving, Newton's second law suggests that the greater mass of the wall exerts force on the lesser object—in this case, the ball—sending the ball flying back at the player. Newton's third law suggests that due to the mass of the concrete wall, it remains stationary when the ball strikes, but the kinetic energy of the ball is redirected in the reverse direction as an equal and opposite reaction. The speed of the ricochet is relative to the speed of the original throw, and one thing the player must keep in mind is that the ball will return from the wall more quickly than if another player was throwing it. The wall does not have to wind up and throw the ball, as a partner would. When players train using wall ball, the instantaneous ball return aids in the development of their reflexes. If players hesitate, or are not ready, the ball will shoot right past them.

## Basic Training: Catching, Elasticity, and the Trampoline Effect

The laws of motion outlined in the previous section have implications for catching the ball as well. In wall ball, the concrete barrier against which the ball is thrown returns the ball with a force that is essentially equal and opposite to the force of the throw. When catching a lacrosse ball, the object is to position one's stick so that the ball lands in the head, against the leather netting or mesh. However, the pocket, while considerably softer that concrete, still causes a slight rebound. The rebound is due to what is called the "trampoline effect." The trampoline effect occurs when two objects strike each other, such as a baseball bat hitting a ball, a person jumping on a trampoline, or a lacrosse ball striking the pocket strings of a stick.

The concept of elasticity determines how a lacrosse ball will rebound off any object. Any time two objects collide, the surface of both will be dented or compressed, if only slightly, provided the objects are not absolutely inflexible. The more elastic an object is, the faster it resumes its original shape, and the more one object will bounce off the other. A baseball bat and ball both possess elasticity, despite their perceived hardness, and so, when they collide, the object with less mass—the ball—goes flying. When the lacrosse ball lands in the pocket of the stick, the pocket strings have an equal and opposite reaction to the ball's energy. While the pocket's elasticity does not approach that of, say, a trampoline, the ball will nevertheless bounce straight out of the pocket if the player is not skilled.

With traditional lacrosse heads in particular, the rigidity of the lacrosse head can cause problems for the player, especially in the women's game where the pocket is shallower than in the men's. The stiffer the material of the head and the tighter the pocket strings, the more the impact with the ball causes the trampoline effect that can make the ball hard to catch. When there is little "give" in the pocket, the ball will simply bounce out of the lacrosse head unless the player is adept at controlling it. Beginner players often struggle with this problem, though even very young players say that with a little training and a bit of eye-hand coordination, catching quickly becomes fairly natural.

*Catching a lacrosse ball requires practice and a bit of finesse.*

Coach David Pietramala counsels players on how to lessen the trampoline effect by pulling the stick back slightly as the ball arrives, "just as he would if he were catching a raw egg to make sure it doesn't break."[62] The player must withdraw the stick adeptly, Pietramala adds, or the trampoline effect will cause the ball to rebound rather than to land softly in the stick and nestle in the pocket.

In girls' lacrosse, especially at the beginner's level, catching the ball can be daunting at first. Coach Jeffrey Rogers, who works with modified girls' lacrosse in Henrietta, New York, observes that the shallow pocket often functions like a tennis racket, deflecting balls away. Rogers believes the remedy is to modify beginner girls' lacrosse sticks, loosening the strings and deepening the pockets to make it easier to catch the ball.

Chapter 4

# Common Lacrosse Injuries

Injuries are a common problem in every sport—from golf to football—and lacrosse is no exception. The levels of exertion, physical contact, and speed during a game all factor into the possibility of bodily injury to participants. As renowned sports surgeon Dr. James Andrews bluntly stated, "Lacrosse is one rough sport."[63]

Former collegiate player and current youth coach Thomas Schmitz called lacrosse a sport of "controlled violence."[64] He recalled an incident that occurred in a men's lacrosse league where a midfielder and a defenseman were battling pretty hard. The defensive player's stick broke off, and one piece caught the midfielder's arm and tore it open so that it was bleeding profusely. Schmitz was trained in first aid, so he took a towel and wrapped it around the player's arm, even as some players were calling for him to apply a tourniquet, which is used to stop excessive bleeding. However, Schmitz waved them off and had them call an ambulance. "The player went to the hospital and got thirty stitches. Then he was back playing with a bandaged arm the next week. Lacrosse players are tough,"[65] Schmitz concluded.

However, lacrosse is not as brutal as some would believe. "[To] the uninitiated …" David G. Pietramala wrote, "lacrosse is a wild, stick-swinging game, [but] it is not nearly as rough as it appears."[66] There are not as many injuries as in football, for example. "Even though body and stick checks are part of [men's] lacrosse, there are definite limitations on them that prevent injuries. In addition, the protective equipment worn by the lacrosse player minimizes injuries."[67] Though officials enforce rules, such as no slashing (swinging the stick at an opponent), that are designed to keep the game as safe as possible, injuries are inevitable. As coach Jim Hickson and journalist Joe Lombardi wrote, "If you play lacrosse, you will get injured."[68]

*Lacrosse is an aggressive sport, one that some have called "controlled violence."*

## Inter-crosse: A Safer Alternative

Inter-crosse, (also called as soft-crosse, mod-crosse, or inter-lacrosse) is an alternative, non-contact form of lacrosse. It features its own set of rules and uses modified lacrosse equipment. Inter-crosse is popular in many European countries (particularly the Czech Republic), as well as in Quebec, Canada. The official version of the sport was started in the 1980s by the Fédération Internationale d'Inter-Crosse and was influenced by pacifism and feminism as a safer alternative to the more violent sport of field lacrosse.

Inter-crosse uses an aluminum and plastic stick and a soft rubber ball. It stresses fair play and is guided by four principles: respect, movement, communication, and adaptability. Inter-crosse also emphasizes enjoyment and participation. Its philosophy is one of inclusiveness, where all players are welcome regardless of physical size, age, gender, or ability. It is often played by younger athletes who will one day transition to field lacrosse.

## Fast Break!

Stretching before a workout or game is one of the most effective ways to reduce injuries such as sprains, strains, and tears.

## When Most Injuries Occur

Some lacrosse scenarios are particularly dangerous. According to Alan McLiverty, a Rochester chapter US Lacrosse president and longtime lacrosse official, "Lacrosse only gets ugly and kids most often get hurt when the ball's on the ground."[69] This is especially true for younger players, who have not yet developed the finesse to pick up the lacrosse ball with the stick while on the run. When the ball is on the ground, players tend to converge and create a scrum—a clustered group of players trying to obtain a loose ball. In such cases, McLiverty said, officials try to "find a push"[70] so that they may blow the whistle and award the ball to the non-offending team. The longer the ball is on the ground, McLiverty said, the more likelihood of an injury.

Some of the more intense injuries in lacrosse include twisted ankles, broken collarbones, anterior cruciate ligament (ACL) and medial collateral ligament (MCL) tears, and concussions. McLiverty stated concussions often occur when players converge in scrums and bang heads, and this is the "number one reason to get the ball off the ground."[71] So important is this official's duty, McLiverty said, that even if a foul is slight, referees will often blow the whistle to end the scrum. Officials use their best judgment in such situations, as player safety is paramount.

*Lacrosse is most dangerous when the ball is on the ground.*

## Twisted Ankles

Dr. James Andrews observes that "strains and sprains are common among lacrosse players."[72] He cites studies showing that "ankle sprains represent roughly 21 percent of all reported injuries for girls and 16 percent for boys at the scholastic [high school] level."[73]

The ankle consists of three bones: The tibia and fibula are long bones that make up the shin; the talus is a small bone that forms a ball-and-socket joint at the base of the tibia and fibula. Ligaments, or fibrous connective tissue, attach the three bones at the joints. The ligaments may stretch and even

*Because lacrosse involves a lot of cutting and dodging, ankle sprains are common.*

tear when players cut and dodge, when they plant their feet awkwardly, when the ground is uneven, or when players' feet come in contact with the feet of other players.

The most common form of ankle sprain is called an inversion, where the ankle rolls outward. Less frequent are eversions, where the ankle rolls inward. There are also three grades of sprains: Grade 1 results when there is slight tearing of the ligament or ligaments. Grade 2 occurs when there is a partial tearing of the ligament or ligaments. Grade 3 is a complete tear of one or more ligaments.

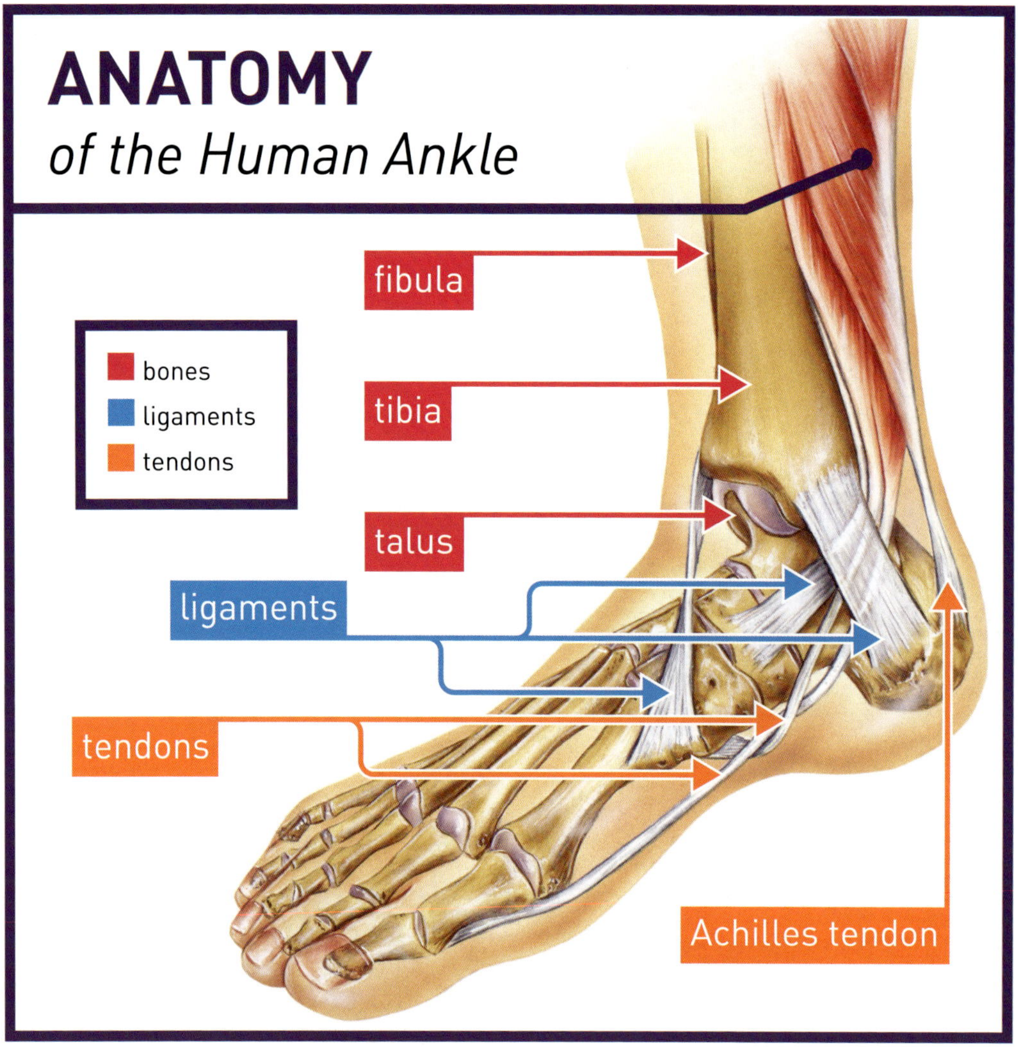


*Shown here is a diagram of the three bones that make up the ankle: the fibula, tibia, and talus. Ligaments and tendons also come together to connect parts of the ankle.*

Treatment for a sprained ankle typically involves the R.I.C.E. method: rest, ice, compression, and elevation. Players who sustain ankle sprains should stay off the foot for at least a week or two. More severe sprains can keep an athlete off the field for a month or more. Grade 2 sprains often require the athlete to wear an elastic bandage or air splint. Grade 3 sprains require a splint, cast, or brace to immobilize the ankle. Surgery may be necessary to reconstruct a completely torn ligament, but, fortunately, this scenario is quite rare.

## Fast Break!

Lacrosse is considered a moderate risk sport. The vast majority of injuries are minor strains, bruises, and sprains; however, major injuries do occur as well.

### Broken Collarbones

The clavicle, or collarbone, is susceptible to breaking in all contact sports, lacrosse included. The clavicle is "the bone that runs horizontally between the top of your breastbone (sternum) and shoulder blade (scapula). The clavicle … helps connect the arm to the body. [One] can feel it by touching the area between [one's] neck and … shoulder. Most people can see the clavicle beneath the skin when they look in the mirror."[74] According to lacrosse historian Thomas Vennum Jr., "Broken collarbones were particularly common"[75] in Native American games of the 19th century and before.

> *Players were frequently tossed into the air by opponents, causing them to land headfirst on the ground. To avoid serious damage to the head or a broken arm, Cherokee players would instinctively hold their head to one side and extend their arms horizontally as they fell, but in doing so they risked breaking their collarbone … To treat the fracture native doctors blew a decoction of poplar bark on the injured man's shoulder and breast and advised him to keep his arm suspended at a 45-degree angle in front of his chest until it healed.*[76]

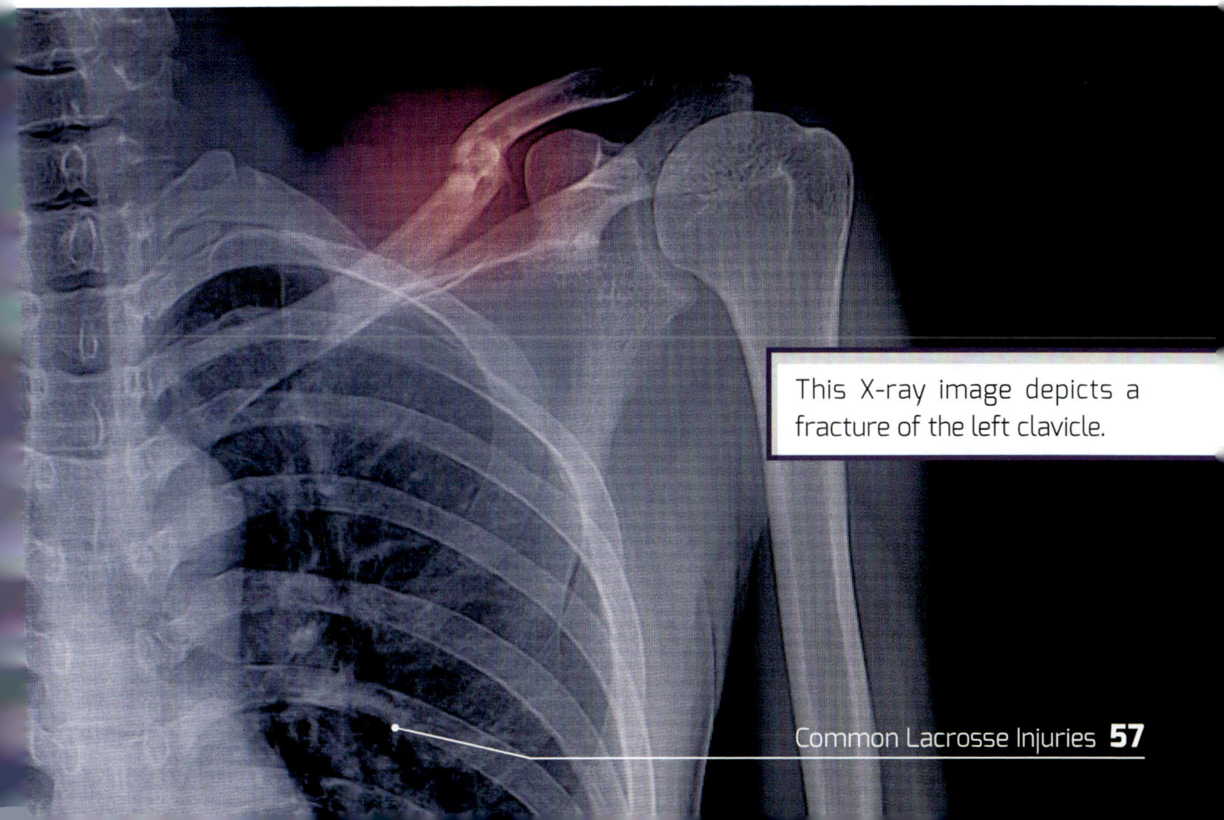

This X-ray image depicts a fracture of the left clavicle.

Despite today's medical advances, treatment for a broken clavicle is not much different. Unless the break is severe, most of these fractures heal without surgery. A shoulder sling, ice, and ibuprofen or acetaminophen is the usual prescription for a broken collarbone.

## *Paul Rabil Discusses Playing While Injured*

In October 2015, Paul Rabil of the New York Lizards wrote a piece for *The Players' Tribune*, an online magazine written by athletes, in which he discussed the risks and rewards of playing while injured. Athletes often play hurt, he said, such as when they play through a sprained ankle or a gash that requires stitches. However, playing through an injury such as "a concussion, a broken bone, or a muscle tear,"[1] can threaten an athlete's career.

Late in the 2014 season, Rabil suffered a Jones fracture in his foot, an injury that has affected other superstars such as basketball's Kevin Durant and football's Dez Bryant. He had season-ending surgery and underwent an extensive rehab schedule, but when he returned for the 2015 season, medically cleared to play, he could tell something was wrong: His foot still hurt.

An X-ray in the middle of the 2015 season showed Rabil had re-broken the foot. However, his team was on the verge of a championship, and he did not want to sit out. Having access to expert medical trainers, Rabil made the agonizing decision to play through the pain. Only a screw that had been put in by surgeons the year before was holding the fracture together. If it broke under the pressure of Rabil's dodges and shots, his career might have ended.

Fortunately, Rabil's foot held up, and the Lizards won the championship. He was operated on three days later.

Rabil knew the risks of playing. As an adult and a professional athlete, he was able to weigh the pros and cons and make the decision for himself. Younger athletes have to be guided in such choices by parents, coaches, and doctors, and they should never play while injured.

1. Paul Rabil, "Playing Injured." *The Players' Tribune*. October 15, 2015. www.theplayerstribune.com/paul-rabil-lacrosse-playing-injured/.

## Knee Injuries

Most injuries occur during scrums for the ball, but knee injuries are an exception. While getting caught in a pile of players can cause a knee to twist in an awkward direction, the most dreaded of knee injuries—the torn ACL—often occurs when there is no contact at all. Many players have torn their ACL merely by planting their foot and changing direction suddenly. As former star player and current Loyola University Maryland coach Jen Adams recalled, "I planted, like I've done 17 billion times before, and … felt it go. It felt like I'd broken a bone in my shin."[77] The ACL tear is a very common lacrosse injury, especially in women's lacrosse. This injury is feared above all others because if a player tears that small ligament, surgery is often a necessity, and the player will typically miss anywhere from nine months to more than a year.

The knee is a hinge joint. It connects the upper leg bone (femur) to the lower leg bone (tibia). The knee "is made up of bones, ligaments, tendons, cartilage, and a joint capsule, all of which are composed of collagen. Ligaments connect bone to bone. Tendons attach muscle to bone. Cartilage is the smooth, fibrous connective tissue covering bones that allows easy, gliding movement. Collagen is the fibrous protein constituent of connective tissue present throughout the body."[78] Additionally, "There are four major ligaments in the knee: the anterior cruciate ligament, posterior cruciate ligament, medial collateral ligament, and lateral (fibular) collateral ligament."[79] All four can suffer sprains or tears, but the ACL is the only ligament that is "entirely within the knee joint."[80] It is "bathed in synovial fluid," and, for this reason, "blood has a harder time reaching the ACL to allow for healing. When blood cannot reach a part of the body, that part will not heal effectively."[81]

When a player plants a foot on the ground and attempts to rotate their body with their entire body weight on the leg, the motion "creates a twisting force across the knee joint, which the ACL must absorb. When the ACL cannot cope with that force, it ruptures."[82] When this occurs, a player's season is over.

About "70 percent of all traumatic knee injuries are of the anterior cruciate ligament."[83] Other common traumatic knee problems include fractures (broken bones), meniscal injuries to the cushioning tissue between the tibia and patella, dislocation, and sprain or rupture of the other three ligaments. Repetitive knee injuries, occurring from repeated motions over time, include tendinitis, bursitis, and runner's knee (patellofemoral syndrome), which are all inflammations, and often treated with anti-inflammatory drugs.

### Fast Break!

Men's lacrosse was a summer Olympic sport in 1904 and 1908 with the only competing teams being the United States (in 1904 only), Canada, and Great Britain. Both times, Canada won gold.

# ANATOMY
*of the Human Knee*

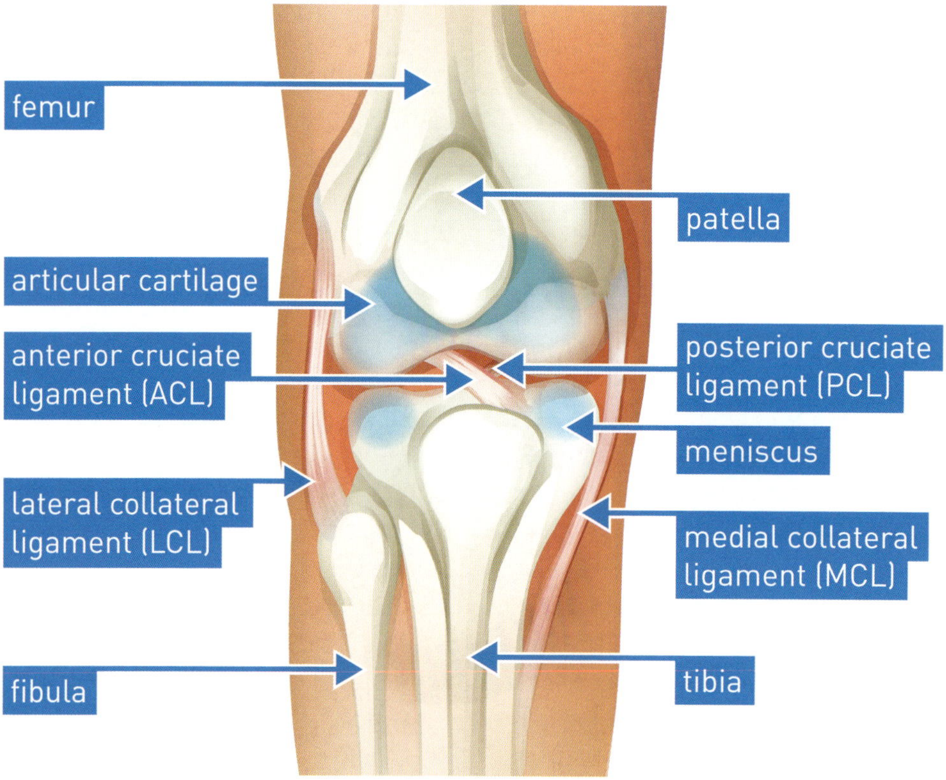


*This diagram shows different parts of the knee. Injuries to the anterior cruciate ligament (ACL) and medial collateral ligament (MCL) are both common in lacrosse.*

## Concussions

As medical knowledge and technology advances in the 21st century, concussions have become a point of growing concern in sports. Football is now realizing the repercussions of repeated concussions, and most sports have enacted concussion protocols designed to protect players. Scientists are studying chronic traumatic encephalopathy, or CTE, a progressive degenerative disease found in many ex-football players who have suffered repeated blows to the head. Now, when players appear to be concussed, they must first pass a series of neurological tests before returning to the game. In soccer, authorities are studying the effects of heading the soccer ball. In women's lacrosse, a debate is now raging over whether to mandate the wearing of helmets during games.

According to Boston University brain researcher Nate Fritts, one does not have to be knocked unconscious or be the victim of one of those huge, spectacular NFL-style hits that make highlight reels to suffer a concussion. "A concussion" Fritts wrote, "occurs anytime you have a hit or jolt to the head that causes you to experience symptoms for any amount of time–even if it is for only a few seconds. The symptoms can include blurred or double vision, seeing stars, sensitivity to light or noise, headache, dizziness or balance problems, nausea, vomiting, trouble sleeping, fatigue, confusion, difficulty remembering, difficulty concentrating, or loss of consciousness."[84] Additionally, some of these symptoms may show up well after the hit, even days after. It is becoming more common for athletes who sustain a head injury to undergo a magnetic resonance imaging (MRI) scan, according to Scott Wilber, a radiologist who played lacrosse at Williams College. Such scans are used to look for internal bleeding. Fortunately, in Wilber's experience, the scans he sees from athletic injuries are "almost always normal."[85]

Concussions are not as common in lacrosse as in football, but they do occur, typically through helmet-to-helmet contact, as when two players vying for a ground ball collide or when a player checks another, often defenseless, player. A 2012 study found that concussion rates in lacrosse are relatively high: Only football and ice hockey, among 20 sports studied, had higher rates of concussions. The study observed that in the case of a defenseless player—that is, one who is unable to protect himself in a particular situation—penalties were not always called: In only "19 out of the 34"[86] observed instances was the offending player penalized for a foul.

*Scientists have developed methods to monitor blows to the head in lacrosse using computer programs.*

Lacrosse officials have been looking for ways to reduce concussions. Computer programs have been developed that can monitor the severity and frequency of blows to the head by linking sensors in players' helmets to computer programs. Rule changes are another weapon against brain trauma. In July 2013, for example, the National Federation of State High School Associations (NFHS) ruled that a check that targets a player in a defenseless position is illegal.

## Lacrosse Deaths

On rare occasions, there have been deaths in lacrosse, which are generally associated with a condition called commotio cordis. Lacrosse organizations such as US Lacrosse have been studying this phenomenon in order to save the lives of affected players. In September 2009, the medical journal *Pediatrics* released a study that surveyed 28 years of data in a registry maintained by the Minneapolis Heart Institute Foundation. They counted 23 incidents of "sudden-death

*Defibrillators can save lives on the rare occasions that a player experiences commotio cordis.*

events"[87] between 1980 and 2008. In 19 cases, the subjects died of cardiac arrest, and 4 players survived the episode.

According to *Lacrosse Magazine*, "Commotio cordis occurs when an individual receives a blow to the chest in a very precise spot over the heart at a very precise moment in the cardiac cycle. The blunt blow—which doesn't even need to have extreme force—imparts an electric charge to the heart, causing ventricular fibrillation in an otherwise normal heart."[88]

Despite the rarity of commotio cordis, US Lacrosse has taken the issue seriously, "bringing together leading researchers, medical experts, and equipment manufacturers"[89] to address the problem. The *Pediatrics* study suggested three important steps to reduce death from commotio cordis. They include the development of a more effective chest protector, the availability of defibrillators (also known as AEDs) at all athletic events, and a public education campaign.

Chapter 5

# Mind Over Matter: The Psychology of Lacrosse

Lacrosse players not only have their physical strength tested, but also their mental strength. Both their mind and body need to be up for any challenges that may arise on the field. One of the most common challenges is fatigue, which can slow down a player and negatively affect their performance. It is also crucial for players to maintain "mental toughness" throughout a game to insure they stay focused. Each player has a different method for staying in the present and combating these mental and physical intrusions.

## Fatigue and the Brain

Ask any lacrosse player or coach for advice on training for an upcoming lacrosse season, and the answer will be similar—do not coast, and always do your best. When Lacrosse AllStars asked some of the best players in the game what advice they would give themselves in high school knowing what they know now, Kyle Harrison of the Ohio Machine said, "Growing up as a player, and especially in high school, I had a tendency to coast through games and practice. I'd tell myself to go as hard as you can, for as long as you can. Don't hold ANYTHING back."[90]

Given that advice, a lacrosse player is bound to get very tired during both training and games. The traditional view on athletic fatigue holds that the body runs on fuel—mainly oxygen (aerobically),

*Lacrosse players are continually on the run. Scientists are looking at ways for players to overcome fatigue.*

but when oxygen begins to get depleted, the body runs on glucose (anaerobically). These fuels power the athlete until they begin to run out, or when by-products of glucose use (lactic acid) build up in the muscles. Therefore, the body is like a car running on gasoline, and when the tank is empty, the body begins to break down and fatigue sets in.

However, what if the automobile analogy is not accurate? Author Mark McClusky cites the examples of runners and bicyclists who go out for a workout, train really hard, but hit the wall (or run out of gas) with several miles to go. They act as if they cannot go a foot farther, and "slog along,"[91] feeling as if they are in survival mode. However, suddenly, with a mile or two to go, they become reenergized, pick up speed, and complete the remainder of the workout at a clip that is by far faster than they moved all day. "Exercise physiologists have a name for that sudden burst of speed and energy at the end of a bout of exertion," McClusky wrote. "They call it the 'end spurt.'"[92] Most athletes have experienced this final surge at one time or another.

If scientist A.V. Hill's theory that the athlete is like an automobile that can operate until its fuel runs out is true, what accounts for end spurt? According to South African scientist and former competitive rower Tim Noakes, there is more operating than just physiology. Noakes and other scientists have proposed the "central governor theory" of fatigue, which poses that "the key factor isn't in the muscles. They argue that activity is controlled by the brain, which has just one goal: to make sure that nothing in our body is pushed beyond the normal range."[93]

There is, however, no empirical evidence to support the central governor theory. For this reason, and because it flies in the face of the traditional understanding of fatigue, the central governor theory is highly controversial. However, if Noakes and other scientists are right that fatigue is a symptom of the brain's desire to keep athletes from injuring themselves by competing too hard, are there psychological ramifications here for athletes, specifically fatigued lacrosse athletes? Noakes, ever the believer in mind over matter, said,

> *The winning athlete is the one whose illusionary symptoms [of fatigue and exhaustion] interfere the least with actual performance—in much the same way that the most successful golfer is the one who does not consciously think when playing any shot.*
>
> *In contrast, athletes who finish behind the winner may make the conscious decision not to win, perhaps even before the [competition] begins. Their deceptive symptoms of "fatigue" may then be used to justify that decision. So the winner is the athlete for whom defeat is the least acceptable rationalization.*[94]

There are coaches in Canada and Great Britain who have begun to design training with Noakes's ideas in mind, and some were even used by athletes training for the 2016 Summer Olympic Games in Brazil. However, the success of these methods and the precise exercises that will use the mind to best enhance athletic performance are still unknown.

One running coach, Jeff Gaudette, has designed an exercise that attempts to overcome the central governor—the mental barrier limiting an athlete's ability to perform. He calls this exercise a hammer interval session.

Such an exercise also lends itself to running workouts for lacrosse. The idea is to run a set of eight intervals: eight runs of an equal distance—656 feet (200 m), for example. Most athletes who do so often run fastest during the first and last intervals. However, Gaudette instructs athletes to run the fourth and seventh intervals the hardest, to "hammer them." Gaudette wrote, "The specific pace of the hammer repeat isn't the important part of this workout. Rather, it's the ability to chip away at the mental constraints late in a workout or race that tell you that you can't go any faster."[95]

The central governor theory is highly controversial and largely untested. However, supporters believe that ideal training methods should allow athletes to overcome the limitations of their minds to achieve maximum performance.

## Sports Psychologists

Sports psychology is the study of how psychology influences athletic performance, exercise, and physical activity. It is an interdisciplinary science that draws on knowledge from many related fields, including biomechanics, physiology, kinesiology, and psychology. Applied sports psychology deals with the athletes themselves, using scientific research to enhance performance on the field.

Employed in this field of study are sports psychologists. They are health professionals who work with athletes to diagnose and treat various types of mental and emotional disorders, including anxiety and stress. Their job description may include working with athletes, coaches, and parents regarding injury, rehabilitation, communication, team building, and career transitions. Sports psychologists may work with an entire team or with an individual athlete. They help athletes maximize their athletic talent by building up their confidence and mental toughness to deal with setbacks and failure.

Sports psychology is a growing field of study. An increasing number of colleges and universities have programs in the field, and an official professional organization, the Association for Applied Sports Psychology (AASP), offers certification in the field.

## Mental Toughness

The greatest athletes in any sport—from Michael Jordan to Michael Phelps to Gary Gait—demonstrated a level of mental strength that matched their physical abilities. Michael Jordan famously hated to lose anything from card games to ping-pong matches. Michael Phelps used to set two alarm clocks at night, one digital and one analog, so that if there was a power outage during the night he would not miss his 5:00 a.m. wakeup call to get ready for swim practice. After his Syracuse women's lacrosse team lost to perennial powerhouse Northwestern, Coach Gait was quick to identify the problem, and it was not physical prowess: "We have to go back and work on our mental toughness and build our confidence up a little more," he said, "so when we get into a game like this and get opportunities, we're able to relax and finish easy opportunities. We'll continue to work on it."[96] Gait knew what he was talking about, having won three NCAA lacrosse championships while a player at Syracuse.

Mental toughness often begins with optimism and confidence. Athletes must believe in themselves. Reinforcement can come from outside—from coaches, parents, or friends—but nothing is more important to the athlete than self-confidence. "Where does confidence come from?" asked Duke University professor of sports psychology and sports ethics Gregory Dale. "It only ultimately comes from yourself."[97]

Successful athletes may not always be the most innately talented. However, the great athletes have to believe in their talent. They have found "a way to be great by focusing on what [they] could do rather than using … limitations as an excuse for failure,"[98] said Bob Rotella, former director of sports psychology at the University of Virginia.Rotella has told the story of a lacrosse player on his team when he coached at the University of Connecticut (UConn): "We had a player I will simply call Larry, and he was perhaps the slowest lacrosse player I had ever seen. Slower than death."[99] Because of this, Coach Rotella made sure that Larry never played much.

### Fast Break!

Sports psychologists suggest athletes prepare for a game by visualizing a successful performance before they take the field, imagining themselves running, shooting, and scoring.

The next year, after Rotella had left UConn, he heard that Larry had broken the school scoring record. He called the coach to confirm the rumor. "Yes, he said. It turned out that Larry was slow of foot, but he had quick hands. So … UConn stationed him at crease attack, where he didn't have to move too much."[100] Larry still looked unimpressive, so the other teams did not guard him closely. They double-teamed other players, so that Larry was often wide open in front of the opponent's goal. "He'd get a pass and use those quick hands to flick the ball into the net." The lesson? "I said to myself, 'Rotella, don't ever think you know what talent looks like. You don't.'"[101]

As Rotella's anecdote suggests, not everyone will recognize an athlete's gifts. However, if athletes have confidence and the will to persevere, they may just end up surprising everyone.

## Failing Well Through Perseverance

Mental toughness also shows itself in how an athlete handles adversity. As Gregory Dale tells lacrosse players, "Some of you like to put on a great show and show everybody how upset you are with yourself,"[102] after making a poor play or a mistake on the field. However, he said, "The only thing you do when you do that is demonstrate your lack of mental toughness. It takes a much more mentally tough athlete [to] deal with the mistake, get your head up,

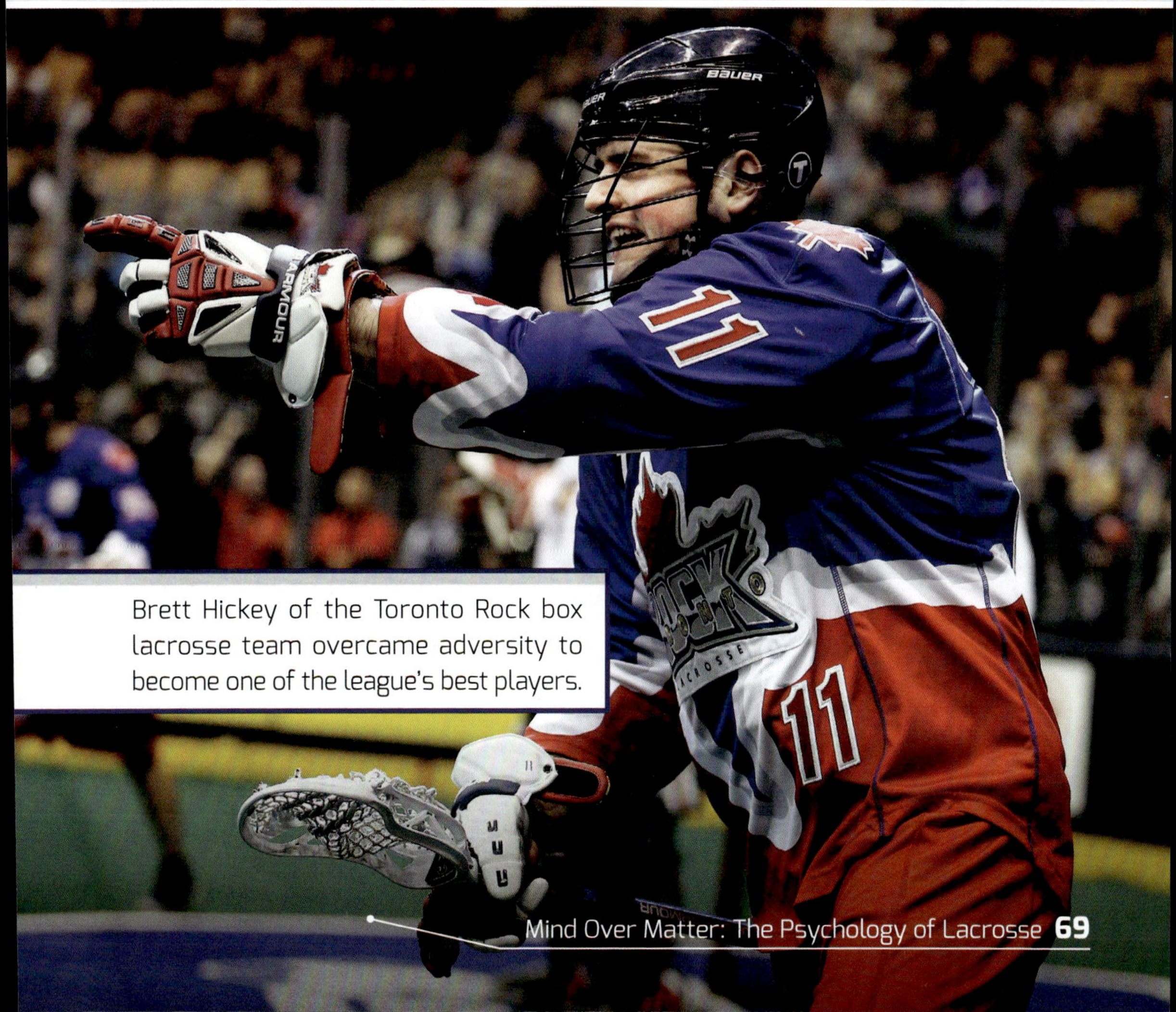


Brett Hickey of the Toronto Rock box lacrosse team overcame adversity to become one of the league's best players.

and make a great play on the next play. *That* is a mentally tough athlete."[103]

Do great athletes fail sometimes? Of course they do. However, how an athlete handles failure makes all the difference. Brett Hickey of the NLL provides one such example. In 2014, the Vancouver Stealth, the team he had played for on and off, asked him to take a demotion to the practice squad. Hickey, who had scored five goals and had five assists playing sporadically for the Stealth, refused the demotion and went home. He considered becoming a police officer, like his father. Instead, he summoned his inner reserves. He began working out in the gym, adding 25 pounds (11.3 kg) of muscle. At 6 foot 2 inches (1.8 m) tall and 225 pounds (102 kg), the Toronto Rock offered him another chance to play box lacrosse. In 2015, the one-time average player scored 50 goals, breaking the Rock record for goals in a season and finishing fourth in the league. He lives by his own motto: "Failure is good. You learn from failure. But fail today because you don't want to fail on game day."[104]

Dr. Kevin Sheehan of Molloy College wrote, "Our history is defined by famous failures from Steve Jobs to Walt Disney to Thomas Edison, Oprah and most recently, Tom Brady. All of these American legends *failed well*, refusing to let failure define them and rededicating their lives with greater effort after initial disappointment." Sheehan believes in the concept of failing well: "We all *fail*. Think back to riding a bike, learning to swim or doing long division, we all failed at first, got back up, took some coaching, put in more effort and ultimately succeeded. After a few bumps and bruises, we all rode the bike."[105]

He goes on to say:

> *We need to teach our students to* fail well *and accept failure as the learning experience that it truly is. Children need to know that they do not have to be perfect all the time, none of us are. Children need to learn the truth about success. Success is borne of* hard work, *work that is not always pleasant, but work that can define us … What we really need to teach our children is the truth about what is at the heart of success, hard work, and most all, we need to teach our children to fall forward and* fail well.[106]

## Fast Break!

Trevor Tierney is the only goalie to have won an NCAA men's lacrosse championship, an International Lacrosse Federation World Lacrosse championship, and an MLL Steinfeld Cup championship as of 2017.

As former publisher and political commentator Arianna Huffington said, "Failure is not the opposite of success; it's a stepping-stone *to* success."[107]

*Excessive distractions can prevent a goalie from doing the all-important job of making the save.*

## The Psychology of Goaltending

At times, the position of goalie can be the loneliest on the field, and in some regard, it is the most important. For these reasons, many goaltenders feel as if they are on an island. Fear, anxiety, and what psychologists call "interference" can set in. Fear often stems from the goalie's knowledge that they may get hit with the ball—which hurts—or injured on a play. Anxiety is characterized as nervousness: the worry that the keeper may give up a goal, among other concerns. Interference involves anything outside of a goalie's main job, which is to guard

## Lacrosse Rituals and Superstitions

While some people might view rituals and superstitions as silly wastes of time, they can actually help athletes focus before a game. These diversions actually go back to the Native Americans, who had numerous rituals before lacrosse games. Many would paint their faces and bodies, just as they would before going to war. Native players often decorated their sticks with symbolic objects that represented qualities desired during a game. There were strict rules about what could and could not be eaten before a game, and medicine men performed rituals to prepare both players and their lacrosse sticks.

Today, rituals and superstitions persist. For some players, listening to a playlist of favorite songs is a must before a game. Stories, often questionable, about players sleeping with their sticks are common. Goalies are a particularly superstitious lot, and some report rituals of tapping the goal posts in different combinations (two taps on left post, one on right, for example) before taking their position in the net. Some teams wear the same color socks during a winning streak and change colors with the first loss.

Several scientific studies have concluded that the real value in superstition or ritual is the confidence boost and the feelings of control that they provide to athletes. If competitors believe that a certain set of actions will improve performance, they often will play better on the field.

against goals being scored. Interference consists of those distracting thoughts that creep in from the outside—about parents, girlfriends or boyfriends, school, or anything besides the next shot on goal.

A goalie's job is singular and simple: Keep the opposing players from scoring. Any of the above thoughts that sneak in while a goalie is in the net are distractions and may lead to a goalie's poor performance. That is where sports psychologists come in.

Chris Buck, a former goalie for Ithaca College, is a certified consultant and member of the Association for Applied Sport Psychology (AASP), as well as the author of *Thinking Inside the Crease.* His book aims to teach goalies how to be mentally tough. He has worked with hundreds of goalies across the country, including those from elite programs such as Johns Hopkins, Syracuse, Notre Dame, University of Pennsylvania, and Georgetown. He has also worked with several MLL professional goalies.

*For a goalie, the next shot is always the most important one.*

Buck believes that the best goalies are those who not only possess outstanding physical tools, but also an exceptional mental game.

Buck teaches goalies how to eliminate anxiety, fear, and interference and to always focus on the game, one play at a time, one shot on goal at a time. He has observed how goalies often manifest fear when an attacking player approaches with the ball and coils up for a shot. This is not an irrational reaction. As former star collegiate and MLL goalie Trevor Tierney said, "If you are a young goalie, and you are scared of the ball, then you are … *smart*! It's a hard rubber ball traveling at an incredibly fast speed, and it is often hitting your body."[108] (Tierney also advocates for better goalie equipment to prevent injuries.)

"If you do feel some fear," Buck said, "your first move is to bring your hands in. The body wants to recoil and protect."[109] This recoiling takes the lacrosse stick out of position, so that it becomes increasingly difficult to make a save. Buck said that when players do this, coaches often "misdiagnose" it as bad form. "But it's not necessarily bad form. It's fear taking over."[110]

Buck suggests that from the moment a goalie steps on the field, he or she must adopt an aggressive, positive, "bring it" mindset. The goalie must keep their hands out in front of the body, find the release point of the shot, and then find the contact point. Absolute concentration is a necessity. Any interference, any fear, any anxiety will cloud the goalie's concentration. When a goalie allows a goal—which is inevitable—the goalie must put it out of mind: The next shot is always more important than the last one. Buck suggests the goalie turn to the goal, get angry for 10 seconds or so, if need be ("emotions are pretty hard to control"[111]), and then let go. Duke Lacrosse has a three-second rule. "You've got three seconds to think about a mistake," said Gregory Dale. "If you're thinking about it any longer than that, you are not mentally tough."[112]

Once the 3 seconds, or 10 seconds, is up, the goalie should turn back to the field and get ready for the next shot. "So it's release the last one and refocus on the next one."[113] "The next shot," Buck stated, "is always, always, always more important than the last one."[114] The goalie needs to take the emotions and the interference out of the game as much as possible. It is simply about stopping a ball, and nothing else. "I want goalie robots," Buck stated. "I want to put them in the cage, and they're always the same. Find the release. Find the contact point. Make the stop."[115]

Chapter 6

# Current Technology and Lacrosse

Lacrosse is a sport steeped in tradition, and traditions tend to have staying power unless good reasons for change are offered. Nevertheless, rapidly advancing technology is a given in the 21st-century world, and though the lacrosse world has been slower than other sports to adopt radical changes, three issues involving technology have taken center stage in the decade of the 2010s. These issues are: helmets in women's lacrosse, a shot clock to limit an offensive team's possession of the ball, and the use of instant replay at the collegiate and professional levels.

## The Women's Helmet Controversy

Proposals to mandate wearing helmets in the women's game have been floated for years, but the controversy over helmets really came to the forefront in 2015, when Florida became the first state to mandate headgear in high school girls' lacrosse. For years, helmets in men's lacrosse have been the norm at all levels of play—from beginners to major leaguers. However, the women's game, with its prohibition of physical contact, has always been viewed as a finesse sport rather than a combative one. Girls and women wear goggles

*Traditionally, only goalies wear helmets in girls' lacrosse. Goggles are mandated for other players.*

during play, but helmets had not been thought necessary to the game. Only women's lacrosse goalies, who face an onslaught of hard rubber balls, have worn helmets.

Opponents of the helmet mandate worry that wearing protective headgear will change the women's game by encouraging a more violent style of play. Helmets might "embolden players to be more aggressive."[116] John Knowles, who coaches girls' lacrosse in the Wayne Central School District in Western New York, worries that wearing helmets will lessen the need to teach lacrosse fundamentals and player safety.

*Some coaches worry wearing helmets will cause girls to be less aware of player safety. Other coaches think helmets will better protect players.*

Instead, he said, coaches may rationalize that "They have helmets, so I don't have to teach stick control anymore."[117]

However, those in favor of the helmet law point out that data shows that girls' lacrosse "has the fifth-highest rate of concussions in high school sports,"[118] behind only football, ice hockey, boys' lacrosse, and girls' soccer. Dawn Comstock, an associate professor of epidemiology (the branch of medicine that deals with diseases and other health factors), published a 2014 report that concluded that boys and girls playing high school lacrosse mostly sustained concussions in different ways. Using her nationally recognized injury database, she concluded that the majority of concussions in boys' lacrosse happened due to athlete-to-athlete collisions (checking, banging heads, etc.), while in girls' lacrosse, concussions largely occurred when players were struck by the ball or a stick.

"Helmets are very good at preventing direct transfer-of-force injuries," Comstock said, such as a blow to the head by a stick or ball. "The girls' lacrosse players are at risk. The question is why girls aren't taking advantage of a part of equipment that boys are taking advantage of."[119]

In the first year of mandated headgear, Florida girls used either soft-shell helmets or, more commonly, flimsy 0.4-inch (10 mm)-thick headbands, which were more like thick bandannas than effective protection. Even so, there is anecdotal evidence that the headbands have had some protective effect.

## A National Standard for Women's Headgear

In 2016, US Lacrosse, the sport's governing body, approved the voluntary use of helmets that met ASTM standards. ASTM International (originally, the American Society for Testing Materials) is an international organization that develops and publishes voluntary consensus technical standards for a wide range of materials, products,

## Rules of Women's Lacrosse

In many sports, the men's and women's game are very similar, sharing many rules and philosophies. This is not true of men's and women's lacrosse. Female lacrosse players like to say that women's lacrosse is a completely different game, one that relies on grace and finesse rather than brute strength.

A key difference concerns the lacrosse stick. Men's pockets are deeper, which allows players to keep control of the ball while absorbing body checks. In women's lacrosse, the pocket is shallow, which makes it more difficult to catch and cradle the ball.

While men can almost pummel each other, women draw a penalty for body checking. Women are allowed to stick check each other, but excessive force will also draw a penalty. Women also do not wear the padding that men do.

The women's field is slightly larger than the men's field, and there are more players (12) than in the men's game. Women's lacrosse is a fast, free-flowing, and often graceful game that prizes ball control, speed, and finesse.

systems, and services. According to the US Lacrosse website, "The ASTM standard is the first-ever performance standard for women's lacrosse headgear, developed to help reduce impact forces associated with stick and ball contact in women's lacrosse."[120]

As for the design of the headgear, US Lacrosse states,

> *The ASTM standard requires the headgear to fully cover the head, thus precluding the use of head band type products currently used by some players. All headgear must be worn with required eyewear, and some headgear models have integrated eyewear. The standard has two options, allowing manufacturers to make their headgear with eyewear implemented or a product that is compatible with various eyewear products currently on the market.*[121]

Certainly creating voluntary helmets will not end the controversy. Nor will it end concussions. Dr. Michael O'Brien, director of the Sports Concussion Clinic at the Micheli Center for Sports Injury Prevention in Massachusetts argues that while helmets may reduce catastrophic injuries, "like skull fracture or intracranial bleed"[122] (bleeding of the brain), they are not much help in reducing the injury many think they are primarily intended for. O'Brien said that "concussions come more from diffuse injury where the brain rotates in the skull,"[123] and helmets are not designed to combat these injuries: "If you think about what happens with what's called rotational acceleration—that's where the brain rotates in the skull either by a moving head that hits an immovable object and the brain spins in the skull, so to speak, or if there's a massive force to the body and there's a rapid whiplash to the head—a helmet can't prevent that type of thing."[124] O'Brien added, "Now if you look at NASCAR, they have an excellent system for trying to reduce that rotational acceleration—like a seat belt for the head and helmet. On the field for an athlete, that's not particularly practical."[125]

## Fast Break!

The Cascade LX helmet, available since November 2016, was the first integrated system to meet international safety standards for women's lacrosse headgear and goggles.

However, for every scientist who claims helmets are not the answer to reducing injury, there will be one who disagrees. Dawn Comstock argues that the gladiator effect—the notion that girls will become more violent if their heads are protected by helmets, "is, in my opinion, a myth that simply will not die—despite the fact that there's not a single piece of published research that I'm aware of that actually proves this idea."[126] Defending the use of protective headgear, she goes on to say, "If it's good enough for the boys, why isn't it good enough to protect girls as well?"[127]

Questions about protective headgear may be purely academic at this point. Inevitably, it seems, the use of helmets will increase in girls' lacrosse, if only because many parents will do anything possible to protect their children. Even if the average cost of the ASTM helmets is more than $100, it is an expense many parents will gladly pay if wearing a helmet prevents even one lacrosse injury.

Penn State and Florida, shown here, have played some hotly contested games.

## Stall-Ball in Women's Lacrosse

In the spring of 2016, the women's lacrosse teams at University of Florida and Penn State University played an NCAA playoff game that was nip and tuck throughout. For most of the game, it was a prime example of everything good that a women's lacrosse game could be. The game featured "thrilling stick-work, hard-nosed defense, and scrappy fights for loose balls,"[128] and had its share of stars: Florida midfielder Nicole Graziano was a finalist for the Tewaaraton trophy (given to the nation's best collegiate player), while Penn State had two All-Americans, with goalie Emi Smith and attacker Madison Cyr. Then, at 53 minutes into the 60-minute contest, the action stopped.

After a Penn State goal tied the game at 13, Florida moved the ball into Penn State's defensive zone and began an almost 7-minute stall. It may have been good strategy (though Penn State did win 14–13 in double overtime), but it was excruciating to watch. The Florida stall was not an isolated occurrence. "Stalling has been in our game too long," said North Carolina coach Jenny Levy. "But I think the amount has gotten worse. It used to be the last 2 to 3 minutes [of a game]. Then you started to see the last 10, stretching into the last 15. Now you're starting to literally see it in the first half."[129]

To end this practice, many NCAA women's lacrosse coaches had advocated for years for a shot clock. Gary Gait, formerly Syracuse University's women's coach, whose team was more than once on the losing side of a stall, was a leading advocate. Gait stated, "The discussion [among coaches] has been that if we wanted to be on TV, we couldn't have a game where a person holds the ball for 10 to 12 minutes in a national championship-type game."[130]

For years, the shot clock, like the concept of protective headgear, was a hard sell among women's lacrosse purists. True women's lacrosse aficionados resisted changes to the women's game that would make it more like men's play. They valued above all things the beauty, grace, and naturalness of the game, and injecting technology such as a shot clock was preposterous to many. It did not help the cause that Gait, the most vocal supporter of the technology, was a man. Nevertheless, big changes were on the way.

## The Advent of the Shot Clock

Athletes and sports fans alike are used to seeing shot clocks and play clocks in sports such as basketball and football. The shot clock in men's lacrosse is a much more recent innovation, but it is increasingly being used at the upper levels of men's and women's lacrosse in order to speed up the game, make it more exciting, and keep it fan friendly. Major league men's lacrosse has, since its inception in 2001, used a

60-second shot clock. The shot clock is reset after each goal, when a shot hits the post, when it is saved by the goalie, or when there is a change of possession. If the clock expires, the other team is granted possession. Teams also have 20 seconds to clear the ball across the midfield line.

## Fast Break!

A complete shot clock system for lacrosse, including two clocks, a controller, and other necessary equipment, can cost between $5,000 and $10,000.

With MLL as a model, NCAA men's lacrosse began to follow suit. In 2013, the rules were changed to prevent stalling. There was no physical shot clock, and calling a stall was left to the officials' discretion. When the officials saw that a team in their offensive zone was not making a good faith effort to attack the net, officials began a 30-second silent countdown. After that period, if the offensive team still had not attempted a shot, they would lose possession of the ball. Most teams did not object to the idea of speeding up the game, but the invisible shot clock was controversial. It placed a lot of pressure on officials to count down the 30 seconds, and, moreover, one official's countdown might be different from another's. There were numerous reports of officials stretching the 30 seconds to 34 or 38.

Consider the Georgetown-Navy contest in 2014. The game went to overtime, and with 2:42 left, the officials called Georgetown for stalling and declared "timer on," forcing the them to shoot within 30 seconds. They should have lost possession of the ball with 2:12 left on the clock. However, Georgetown's winning goal was not released until the clock read 2:08. The goal was allowed to stand.

The result of this fiasco and others like it was the adoption of a physical shot clock. In 2015, the NCAA rules committee met and decided to use a visible shot clock, preferably one at each end of the field, for Division I games. This practice was voluntary in 2015, then mandatory in 2016. Division II and III teams had until 2017 to begin using the shot clock. The clock would still be started when the officials, at their discretion, called a team for stalling.

Women's NCAA lacrosse has gone even further than the men. In 2017 play, Division I women began using a 90-second shot clock, to be started from the time that a team first gains possession. The committee's reason for instituting this rule is "to increase the pace of play, contribute to the growth of the game, allow for better competitive balance between the attack and defense, and improve the safety of the game." They note that rough fouls most frequently "occur when the attacking team is maintaining possession of the ball for an extended duration of time."[131]

Will these shot clock innovations eventually filter down to high school lacrosse and perhaps even younger leagues? The expense of installing the clocks on scholastic fields all over America might loom large, but cost has not stopped every school in the country from having shot clocks on basketball courts, so the possibility certainly exists.

## Instant Replay for Intercollegiate Lacrosse

Instant replay is another technological tool that is finding its way into the lacrosse world, having already made significant inroads in basketball, football, and even the most traditional of American sports, baseball. Football fans have grown accustomed to seeing coaches throw the red flag to challenge an official's call on the field.

As in the other sports, there are numerous concerns about using replay in lacrosse, but it is telling that none of the other sports has dropped the use of replay once it was introduced. A key concern is that replay will slow down "the fastest game on two feet."

Already the professional lacrosse leagues have adopted replay for certain game situations. In 2009, the NLL began using instant replay to review disputed goals and crease violations. Coaches were each allowed two challenges per game. In 2015, the league expanded the allowable challenges to three, provided the coach was successful on the previous two challenges.

## Bill Belichick, Lacrosse Fan

Bill Belichick, arguably the greatest pro-football coach of all time, has won championships with the New York Giants and the New England Patriots. What is less well known is that Belichick grew up playing lacrosse, and all his children have been involved in the sport as well.

Belichick has a reputation for giving one-word answers during New England Patriots press conferences, but get him discussing lacrosse, and he can talk for hours. Belichick played lacrosse in high school and at Wesleyan College in Connecticut. His daughter, Debby Clarke Belichick, also played lacrosse at her father's alma mater and is head lacrosse coach at Holy Cross College in Massachusetts. His son, Steve, played lacrosse at Rutgers University in New Jersey, and his son, Brian, played the sport at Trinity College in Connecticut.

The Belichicks are a family that truly loves football and lacrosse.

*Technology has made instant replay easier and faster in recent years. Its use has impacted many sports.*

Since 2013, MLL has used replay for shots on goal only. Head coaches have red flags, similar to those in the NFL, and are allowed two challenges per game during regulation time. A coach may challenge the validity of a scored goal or a shot on goal that the officials have not credited as a score. In order not to slow the game down too dramatically, officials are allowed a maximum of 90 seconds to review the play and come to a decision.

Much discussion regarding the implementation of replay has taken place among NCAA officials, coaches, players, and fans. In recent years, there have been some high-profile disputed goals that have intensified the clamoring for replay at the intercollegiate level. As an anonymous MLL player said about replay, "I think it is great … especially since I have both scored a goal that did not count and also witnessed a top ten highlight of a goal against us that never crossed the goal line."[132]

Since most regular season games are not televised, the resources to implement replay for all games are simply not there. The NCAA Division I playoffs, on the other hand, have been televised by ESPN, and many in the lacrosse community believe that playoff lacrosse is the perfect setting to begin using replay. University of Maryland lacrosse coach John Tillman is among those coaches in favor of replay. "I think anything that helps the game, I'm all for it," he said. "You're seeing it more in other sports. You're seeing it more in football and baseball. The game's being played, and it's a fast game."[133] Lacrosse shots travel so quickly, sometimes up to more than 100 miles (160 km) per hour, that determining whether a shot is a goal or not can sometimes be impossible with the naked eye. Stony Brook University women's lacrosse coach Joe Spallina, who also coaches MLL's New York Lizards, is also in favor of replay

## Fast Break!

In June 2014, The MLL's Chesapeake Bayhawks defeated the Boston Cannons 16–15 when Boston's game-tying goal was overturned by instant replay.

*Maryland coach John Tillman, shown here, is in favor of instant replay at the NCAA level.*

for the NCAA, having seen it work in the professional league. However, he also understands that tradition dies hard when it comes to lacrosse. "It's great on the MLL level," said Spallina. "I hope people would be receptive to [instant replay]. As you know, a lot of this stuff takes a little bit of time for people to wrap their brains around the new way of lacrosse."[134]

Lacrosse is a traditional sport, which is why instituting changes such as instant replay is not easy. However, it is also a growing sport, and using the latest technology will help it gain popularity in more schools and markets than ever before. In both the most traditional forms of the sport and the most modern, science has always shaped the way lacrosse is played. It governs play on the field, training in the gym, and injury treatment in the training room. By using science and technology to push the sport to new heights, the fastest game on two feet will only get faster and more popular in the future.

# Notes

## Chapter 1: The Fastest Game on Two Feet

1. Sean Lydon, interview with author, August 24, 2016.
2. David G. Pietramala and Neil Grauer, *Lacrosse: Technique and Tradition*. Baltimore, MD: Johns Hopkins University Press, 2006, p. 3.
3. Alexander M. Weyand and Milton R. Roberts, *The Lacrosse Story*. Baltimore, MD: H. & A. Herman, 1965, p. 7.
4. Thomas Vennum, *American Indian Lacrosse: Little Brother of War*. Baltimore, MD: Johns Hopkins University Press, 1994, p. xii.
5. Weyand and Roberts, *The Lacrosse Story*, p. 7.
6. Donald M. Fisher, *Lacrosse: A History of the Game*. Baltimore, MD: Johns Hopkins University Press, 2002, p. 13.
7. Weyand and Roberts, *The Lacrosse Story*, p. 8.
8. Pietramala and Grauer, *Lacrosse: Technique and Tradition*, p. 9.
9. Weyand and Roberts, *The Lacrosse Story*, p. 13.
10. Weyand and Roberts, *The Lacrosse Story*, pp. 16–17.
11. Weyand and Roberts, *The Lacrosse Story*, p. 17.
12. Pietramala and Grauer, *Lacrosse: Technique and Tradition*, p. 11.
13. Pietramala and Grauer, *Lacrosse: Technique and Tradition*, p. 11.
14. Fisher, *Lacrosse: A History of the Game*, p. 70.
15. Fisher, *Lacrosse: A History of the Game*, p. 72.
16. Quoted in Weyand and Roberts, *The Lacrosse Story*, p. 103.

## Chapter 2: The Biomechanics of Lacrosse

17. M. B. Roberts, *Lacrosse: The Player's Handbook*, New York, NY: Sterling Publishing Company, 2007, p. 54.
18. "Equipment for Boys' and Mens' Lacrosse," US Lacrosse. www.uslacrosse.org/safety/equipment/player-equipment.
19. American Sport Education Program, *Coaching Youth Lacrosse*, Champaign, IL: Human Kinetics, 2007, p. 165.

20. John McPhee, "Spin Right and Shoot Left," *The New Yorker*, March 23, 2009. www.newyorker.com/magazine/2009/03/23/spin-right-and-shoot-left.
21. Roberts, *Lacrosse: The Player's Handbook*, p. 58.
22. McPhee, "Spin Right and Shoot Left."
23. Pietramala and Grauer, *Lacrosse: Technique and Tradition*, p. 41.
24. Pietramala and Grauer, *Lacrosse: Technique and Tradition*, p. 16.
25. "The Sport Science of Paul Rabil's Lacrosse Shot Watch Major League Lacrosse on ESPN3.Com," YouTube video, 3:19, posted by ilacrosse, July 24, 2012. www.youtube.com/watch?v=BjiIer6_6Qc.
26. McPhee, "Spin Right and Shoot Left."
27. "The Sport Science of Paul Rabil's Lacrosse Shot," YouTube video, posted by ilacrosse.
28. Frank Vizard, ed. *Why a Curveball Curves: The Incredible Science of Sports*. New York, NY: Hearst Books, 2008, p. 121.
29. "The Sport Science of Paul Rabil's Lacrosse Shot," YouTube video, posted by ilacrosse.
30. Vizard, ed. *Why a Curveball Curves: The Incredible Science of Sports*, p. 121.
31. "Paul Rabil Experience Shooting Tips: Fundamentals and Drills," YouTube video, 11:19, posted by US Lacrosse, October 8, 2015. www.youtube.com/watch?v=ujqm0sdy93M.
32. "The Science of a Lacrosse Goalie," YouTube video, 3:24, posted by Tobii Pro, August 12, 2016. www.youtube.com/watch?v=8eSeN8YnwTU.
33. "The Science of a Lacrosse Goalie," YouTube video, posted by Tobii Pro.
34. "The Science of a Lacrosse Goalie," YouTube video, posted by Tobii Pro.
35. "The Science of a Lacrosse Goalie," YouTube video, posted by Tobii Pro.
36. Alan McLiverty, interview with author, September 14, 2016.
37. "Sport Science: Lacrosse Faceoffs," ESPN video, 2:42. www.espn.com/video/clip?id=12897693.
38. "Sport Science: Lacrosse Faceoffs," ESPN video.

## Chapter 3: Training for Endurance, Agility, and Strength

39. Stephen M. Ross, "Why Does Lactic Acid Build Up in Muscles? And Why Does it Cause Soreness?," *Scientific American*. www.scientificamerican.com/article/why-does-lactic-acid-buil/.
40. Ross, "Why Does Lactic Acid Build Up in Muscles? And Why Does it Cause Soreness?"

41. Quoted in Gina Kolata, "Lactic Acid Is Not Muscles' Foe, It's Fuel," *New York Times*, May 16, 2006. www.nytimes.com/2006/05/16/health/nutrition/16run.html.
42. Kolata, "Lactic Acid Is Not Muscles' Foe, It's Fuel."
43. Kolata, "Lactic Acid Is Not Muscles' Foe, It's Fuel."
44. Mark McClusky, *Faster, Higher, Stronger: How Sports Science Is Creating a New Generation of Superathletes, and What We Can Learn from Them*. New York, NY: Plume, 2014, p. 145.
45. McClusky, *Faster, Higher, Stronger*, p. 144.
46. Vizard, ed. *Why a Curveball Curves: The Incredible Science of Sports*, p. 120.
47. John Zumerchik, *Encyclopedia of Sports Science*. Volume 2. New York, NY: Simon and Schuster Macmillan, 1997, p. 485.
48. Zumerchik, *Encyclopedia of Sports Science*, p. 485.
49. Roberts, *Lacrosse: The Player's Handbook*, p. 118.
50. Donald A. Chu, *Jumping Into Plyometrics*. 2nd ed. Champaign, IL: Human Kinetics, 1998, p. 2.
51. Chu, *Jumping Into Plyometrics*, p. 2.
52. Billy J. Voltaire, "Strength & Conditioning for Lacrosse: Plyometrics (Power Training)," Laxpower. www.laxpower.com/content/voltaire/04_plyometrics.php.
53. Voltaire, "Strength & Conditioning for Lacrosse: Plyometrics (Power Training)."
54. Voltaire, "Strength & Conditioning for Lacrosse: Plyometrics (Power Training)."
55. Chu, *Jumping Into Plyometrics*, p. 111.
56. Voltaire, "Strength & Conditioning for Lacrosse: Plyometrics (Power Training)."
57. David Urick and Heinz Kluetmeier, *Sports Illustrated Lacrosse: Fundamentals for Winning*. New York, N.Y: Sports Illustrated, 1988, p. 34.
58. Pietramala and Grauer, *Lacrosse: Technique and Tradition*, p. 51.
59. Quoted in Jim Lucas, "What Are Centrifugal & Centripetal Forces?," Live Science, October 15, 2015. www.livescience.com/52488-centrifugal-centripetal-forces.html.
60. Scott Wilbur, interview with author, October 25, 2016.
61 Roberts, *Lacrosse: The Player's Handbook*, p. 112.
62. Pietramala and Grauer, *Lacrosse: Technique and Tradition*, pp. 54–55.

## Chapter 4: Common Lacrosse Injuries

63. James R. Andrews, *Any Given Monday*. New York, NY: Scribner, 2013, p. 129.
64. Thomas Schmitz, interview with author, November 9, 2016.
65. Thomas Schmitz, interview with author.
66. Pietramala and Grauer, *Lacrosse: Technique and Tradition*, pp. 35–36.
67. Pietramala and Grauer, *Lacrosse: Technique and Tradition*, p. 36.
68. Jim Hickson and Joe Lombardi, *Lacrosse for Dummies*, 2nd ed. Mississauga, ON: Wiley, 2010, p. 173.
69. Alan McLiverty, interview with author.
70. Alan McLiverty, interview with author.
71. Alan McLiverty, interview with author.
72. Andrews, *Any Given Monday*, p. 130.
73. Andrews, *Any Given Monday*, p. 130.
74. "Clavicle Fracture," Akron Children's Hospital, September 2014. www.akronchildrens.org/cms/kidshealth/dfd3dcd76c620d68/.
75. Thomas Vennum Jr., *American Indian Lacrosse: Little Brother of War*. Washington, D.C.: Smithsonian Institution Press, 1994, p. 227.
76. Vennum Jr., *American Indian Lacrosse: Little Brother of War*, p. 227.
77. Claire Lochary, "ACL Confessions," *Lacrosse Magazine*. www.laxmagazine.com/genrel/101013_acl_confessions_the_most_dreaded_injury_in_lacrosse.
78. Mark Darrow, *The Knee Sourcebook*. Chicago, IL.: Contemporary Books, 2002, pp. 2–4.
79. Robert G. Marx with Grethe Myklebust and Brian W. Boyle, *The ACL Solution*. New York, NY: DemosHEALTH, 2012, p. 4.
80. Marx, Myklebust, and Boyle, *The ACL Solution*, p. 4.
81. Marx, Myklebust, and Boyle, *The ACL Solution*, p. 4.
82. Marx, Myklebust, and Boyle, *The ACL Solution*, p. 5.
83. Darrow, *The Knee Sourcebook*, p. 20.
84. Nate Fritts, "Concussions in Lacrosse: Part 1 of 3," Lacrosse AllStars. laxallstars.com/concussions-in-lacrosse-part-1-of-3/.
85. Scott Wilbur, interview with author.
86. Lindsey Barton Straus, "High Concussion Rate in Boys' Lacrosse Blamed on Intentional Head-to-Head Contact with Defenseless Players," MomsTEAM: The Trusted Source for Sports Parents. www.momsteam.com/health-safety/high-concussion-rate-in-boys-lacrosse-blamed-on-intentional-head-head-contact-and-lax-rules-enforcement#ixzz4KjGXKZGr.

87. Quoted in Lindsey Barton Straus, "Lacrosse Has Highest Death Rate from Ill-Timed Blows to Chest," MomsTEAM: The Trusted Source for Sports Parents. www.momsteam.com/sports/risk-sudden-cardiac-death-from-ill-timed-blow-chest-commotio-cordis-highest-in-lacrosse-hockey.
88. Matt DaSilva, "Rochester Boy Dies After Struck by Lacrosse Ball," *Lacrosse Magazine*, February 7, 2012. laxmagazine.prestosports.com/blogs/author/dasilva/02.07.2012_at_2.30_p.m._by_Matt_DaSilva.
89. DaSilva, "Rochester Boy Dies After Struck by Lacrosse Ball."

## Chapter 5: Mind Over Matter: The Psychology of Lacrosse

90. Quoted in Chris Rosenthall, "The Best Lacrosse Advice You'll Ever Hear," Lacrosse AllStars, February 22, 2013. laxallstars.com/the-best-lacrosse-advice-youll-ever-hear/.
91. McClusky, *Faster, Higher, Stronger*, p. 148.
92. McClusky, *Faster, Higher, Stronger*, p. 148.
93. McClusky, *Faster, Higher, Stronger*, p. 149.
94. Quoted in McClusky, *Faster, Higher, Stronger*, p. 159.
95. Jeff Gaudette, "Mind over Matter? The Central Governor Theory Explained," *Runners Connect*. runnersconnect.net/running-training-articles/central-governor-theory/.
96. Quoted in "Postgame Quotes," Cuse.com. cuse.com/sports/2010/3/21/WLAX_0321104927.aspx?id=6959.
97. "2012 Legacy Lacrosse Cup Key Note Speaker Dr. Gregory Dale, Part 5," YouTube video, 8:50, posted by Sarah Funderburk Weston, May 1, 2012. www.youtube.com/watch?v=mbzrb2_CX80.
98. Bob Rotella, *How Champions Think: In Sports and in Life*. New York, NY: Simon & Schuster, 2015, p. 61.
99. Rotella, *How Champions Think*, p. 59.
100. Rotella, *How Champions Think*, p. 60.
101. Rotella, *How Champions Think*, p. 60.
102. "2012 Legacy Lacrosse Cup Key Note Speaker Dr. Gregory Dale, Part 5," YouTube video, posted by Sarah Funderburk Weston.
103. "2012 Legacy Lacrosse Cup Key Note Speaker Dr. Gregory Dale, Part 5," YouTube video, posted by Sarah Funderburk Weston.
104. Quoted in Curtis Rush, "Brett Hickey's Early Failures in NLL Led to 50-Goal Season with Toronto Rock," thestar.com, January 6, 2016. www.thestar.com/sports/lacrosse/2016/01/06/brett-hickeys-early-failures-in-nll-led-to-50-goal-season-with-toronto-rock.html.

105. Kevin Sheehan, "Learning to Fail Well: What Our Kids Need to Learn Most at the Age of Opting Out," 3dLacrosse. 3dlacrosse.com/blog/learning-fail-well-what-our-kids-need-learn-most-age-opting-out.
106. Sheehan, "Learning to Fail Well: What Our Kids Need to Learn Most at the Age of Opting Out."
107. Quoted in Mark H. Anshel, *In Praise of Failure: The Value of Overcoming Mistakes in Sports and in Life*. Lanham, MD: Rowman & Littlefield, 2016, p. 1.
108. Trevor Tierney, "How to Become a Fearless Goalie," Lacrosse Allstars, April 19, 2012. laxallstars.com/how-to-become-a-fearless-lacrosse-goalie/.
109. "Lacrosse Goalie Psychology—Chris Buck," YouTube video, 59:32, posted by Phil Toran, August 4, 2014. www.youtube.com/watch?v=3_1KrODDgw0.
110. "Lacrosse Goalie Psychology—Chris Buck," YouTube video, posted by Phil Toran.
111. "Lacrosse Goalie Psychology—Chris Buck," YouTube video, posted by Phil Toran.
112. "2012 Legacy Lacrosse Cup Key Note Speaker Dr. Gregory Dale, Part 5," YouTube video, posted by Sarah Funderburk Weston.
113. "Lacrosse Goalie Psychology—Chris Buck," YouTube video, posted by Phil Toran.
114. "Lacrosse Goalie Psychology—Chris Buck," YouTube video, posted by Phil Toran.
115. "Lacrosse Goalie Psychology—Chris Buck," YouTube video, posted by Phil Toran.

## Chapter 6: Current Technology and Lacrosse

116. Bill Pennington, "Headgear Rule for Girls' Lacrosse Ignites Outcry," *New York Times*, March 30, 2015. www.nytimes.com/2015/03/31/sports/in-girls-lacrosse-a-move-in-the-name-of-safety-sparks-debate.html?_r=1.
117. John Knowles, interview with author, November 11, 2016.
118. Pennington, "Headgear Rule for Girls' Lacrosse Ignites Outcry."
119. Quoted in Pennington, "Headgear Rule for Girls' Lacrosse Ignites Outcry."
120. US Lacrosse, "Womens Lacrosse Headgear FAQ." www.uslacrosse.org/safety/equipment/womens-lacrosse-headgear-faq.
121. US Lacrosse, "Womens Lacrosse Headgear FAQ."

122. Quoted in Michael O'Brien, "Expert Says: Helmets Won't Reduce Concussions In Girls' Lacrosse," *Only a Game*, April 4, 2015. www.wbur.org/onlyagame/2015/04/04/helmets-girls-lacrosse-concussions.
123. Quoted in O'Brien, "Expert Says: Helmets Won't Reduce Concussions In Girls' Lacrosse."
124. Quoted in O'Brien, "Expert Says: Helmets Won't Reduce Concussions In Girls' Lacrosse."
125. Quoted in O'Brien, "Expert Says: Helmets Won't Reduce Concussions In Girls' Lacrosse."
126. Quoted in Dawn Comstock, "Lacrosse Helmets: Good Enough For Boys, Why Aren't Girls Wearing Them?," *Only a Game*. www.wbur.org/onlyagame/2015/04/04/lacrosse-helmets-girls-safety.
127. Quoted in Comstock, "Lacrosse Helmets: Good Enough For Boys, Why Aren't Girls Wearing Them?"
128. Matt White, "The End of an Era in Women's Lacrosse: Say Goodbye to the Stall," ESPNW. May 25, 2016. www.espn.com/espnw/sports/article/15679649/the-end-era-women-lacrosse-say-goodbye-stall.
129. Quoted in White, "The End of an Era in Women's Lacrosse: Say Goodbye to the Stall."
130. Quoted in White, "The End of an Era in Women's Lacrosse: Say Goodbye to the Stall."
131. "A Look at the Women's Game: NCAA Approves Possession Clock," 3dLacrosse. 3dlacrosse.com/blog/look-womens-game-ncaa-approves-possession-clock.
132. Quoted in Connor Wilson, "Major League Lacrosse Introduces Instant Replay in 2013," Lacrosse Allstars, September 5, 2012. laxallstars.com/major-league-lacrosse-introduces-instant-replay-in-2013/.
133. Quoted in Mike Preston, "Maryland-Yale Finish Latest Example of Why College Lacrosse Needs Instant Replay," *Baltimore Sun*, May 12, 2015. www.baltimoresun.com/sports/bs-sp-preston-lacrosse-column-0513-20150512-column.html.
134. Quoted in Meghan Schneider, "Florida Non-Goal, PSU Save Stir Discussion of Instant Replay," *US Lacrosse Magazine*, May 20, 2016. laxmagazine.prestosports.com/college_women/DI/2015-16/news/052016_florida_non_goal_penn_state_save_stir_discussion_of_instant_replay.

# Glossary

**acceleration:** A change in the velocity of something.

**attackmen:** The offensive players who operate around the goal area.

**body checking:** The process in which a defensive player makes bodily contact with the offensive player. Body checking is legal in men's lacrosse but not in women's.

**breechcloth:** Cloth worn around thc loins as the only article of clothing; loincloth.

**central governor theory:** The concept that the mind controls physical ability and that it will impede physical performance in order to prevent overexertion.

**centrifugal force:** An apparent force that acts outward on an object moving around a center. Scientists have not found this force to be real, only imagined.

**centripetal force:** A force that acts on an object moving in a circular pattern and is directed toward the center around which the object is moving.

**cradling:** The act of deepening the ball in the head of the stick by rhythmically moving the arms and wrists.

**crease:** A circle with a 9-foot (2.7 m) radius around the goal that offensive players cannot enter.

**decoction:** A drink made by boiling herbal or plant material, which may include stems, roots, or bark.

**dodging:** The act of faking out or eluding a defensive player.

**draw:** The play used to start a women's lacrosse game (and after goals). It is the equivalent of the men's face-off. The players hold the ball between the heads of the sticks and draw the ball upward, attempting to control it.

**force:** An interaction that changes the motion of an object.

**ground ball:** A loose ball that neither team controls. Balls can become ground balls after a shot, a bad pass, a face-off, or a check.

**head:** The plastic part of the lacrosse stick that contains the pocket.

**mass:** The property of an object that measures the amount of matter it contains.

**midfielders:** The players who occupy the center of the field and can play on both offense and defense.

**momentum:** Force or speed of movement; the product of the mass and velocity of an object.

**motorcycle grip:** A method of holding the stick with two hands over the top, facing downward, during face-offs; also known as a double over.

**motor unit:** Neurons and muscle fibers that work together to coordinate the contractions of a muscle.

**passing:** The process of throwing the ball to a teammate.

**scrum:** A brief and disorderly struggle or fight for a loose ball.

**stick checking:** The process by which a defensive player tries to impede an offensive player by using the lacrosse stick. Stick checking is legal in both men's and women's lacrosse.

**trampoline effect:** The bouncing back of a ball off another object.

# For More Information

## Books

Fink, Noah, and Melissa Gaskill. *Lacrosse: A Guide for Parents and Players*. Austin, TX: Mansion Grove House, 2006.

This book takes parents and players from the first steps in learning the game of lacrosse through advice on playing the sport in college and lacrosse careers.

Fisher, Donald M. *Lacrosse: A History of the Game*. Baltimore, MD: Johns Hopkins University Press, 2011.

Fisher covers the history of lacrosse—from its beginnings in Native American culture through the 20th century.

Hinkson, Jim. *Lacrosse Fundamentals.* Chicago, IL: Triumph Books, 2012.

As the title suggests, this book covers every aspect of the fundamentals of lacrosse, including passing, cradling, shooting, goaltending, and more.

Pietramala, David G., and Neil Grauer, *Lacrosse: Technique and Tradition*. Baltimore, MD: Johns Hopkins University Press, 2006.

Considered the Bible of lacrosse, this book is an update of Bob Scott's classic by Pietramala, coach at Johns Hopkins University, and Neil Grauer.

Roberts, M. B. *Lacrosse: The Player's Handbook*. New York, NY: Sterling Publishing Co., 2007.

Roberts's book is jammed with insightful advice and tips on how to become a better player. The book is full of pictures illustrating various skills and drills.

Urick, Dave. *Sports Illustrated Lacrosse: Fundamentals for Winning*. New York, NY: Lanham Taylor Trade Publishing, 2008.

This book covers the basics of lacrosse and contains many pictures and diagrams that illustrate fundamental skills of the sport.

Vennum, Thomas. *American Indian Lacrosse: Little Brother of War*. Baltimore, MD: Johns Hopkins University Press, 2008.

This book provides an in-depth look at the beginnings of lacrosse and the sport's importance in Native American culture.

## Websites

**Inside Lacrosse**
**www.insidelacrosse.com**
This website contains lacrosse videos, which include game highlights, recruiting information, fundamental skills, and more.

**Lacrosse Allstars**
**laxallstars.com**
This website offers articles, news, and even podcasts about the game, training, current events, and the business of lacrosse.

**LaxPower**
**www.laxpower.com**
LaxPower contains news of the sport at all levels, including men's, women's, boys', and girls' lacrosse. It is a great resource for team rankings, game calendars, and college recruiting.

**US Lacrosse**
**www.uslacrosse.org**
This is the governing body of lacrosse in the United States. The website contains numerous resources for players of all ages and includes a large section on the rules of the sport.

***US Lacrosse Magazine* Digital Editions**
**www.uslacrosse.org/multimedia/lacrosse-magazine-digital-editions**
This is another site affiliated with US Lacrosse. Digital editions of the print version of *US Lacrosse Magazine* are available at this site. The magazines are filled with articles and high-quality pictures.

***US Lacrosse Magazine* Online**
**www.uslaxmagazine.com**
This magazine site for the US Lacrosse organization focuses on news, including high school, college, professional, and international lacrosse.

# Index

# Picture Credits

Cover Peter Dean/Shutterstock.com; cover, pp. 1, 3, 4, 6, 22, 35, 51, 64, 75, 87, 94, 96, 98, 103, 104 (background) Ekaterina Koolaeva/Shutterstock.com; pp. 4, 6, 22, 35, 51, 64, 75 (lacrosse sticks) nexusby/Shutterstock.com; p. 7 Vladimir Korostyshevskiy/Shutterstock.com; p. 9 courtesy of the Library of Congress; p. 11 Jupiterimages/PHOTOS.com/Thinkstock; p. 13 Kurt Hutton/Picture Post/Getty Images; p. 15 Jim Rogash/WireImage/Getty Images; pp. 16–17 Dejan Popovic/Shutterstock.com; p. 19 Justin Edmonds/Getty Images; p. 20 John Biever/Sports Illustrated/Getty Images; p. 23 Marilyn Angel Wynn/Nativestock/Getty Images; p. 25 poc0loco/iStock/Thinkstock; p. 27 Collegiate Images/Getty Images; p. 28 Marc Serota/Getty Images; pp. 30, 34 Adam Hunger/Getty Images; p. 32 Jim McIsaac/Getty Images; p. 36 James Boardman/Hemera/Thinkstock; p. 37 © istockphoto.com/iacona; p. 41 Syracuse/Collegiate Images/Getty Images; p. 45 Syda Productions/Shutterstock.com; pp. 47, 52 Aspen Photo/Shutterstock.com; p. 50 Brian A. Westerholt/Getty Images; p. 54 Grant Halverson/Getty Images; p. 55 Andy Mead/YCJ/Icon Sportswire via Getty Images; p. 56 Medical Art Inc/Shutterstock.com; p. 57 praisaeng/iStock/Thinkstock; p. 60 BlueRingMedia/Shutterstock.com; p. 61 Gregory Rec/Portland Press Herald via Getty Images; p. 62 Laszlo66/Shutterstock.com; p. 65 Lance King/Getty Images; p. 69 Richard Lautens/Toronto Star via Getty Images; p. 71 jaboardm/iStock/Thinkstock; p. 73 Tim Greenway/Portland Press Herald via Getty Images; p. 76 Alan C. Heison/Shutterstock.com; p. 77 Icon Sportswire via AP Images; p. 80 AP Photo/Centre Daily Times, Abby Drey/MAGS OUT; p. 84 Jamie Sabau/Getty Images; p. 85 Winslow Townson/Getty Images.

# About the Author

**Gary Wiener** is a retired educator, having spent 33 years as an English teacher, department head, assistant principal, and district curriculum leader. He holds a PhD from the University of Rochester and lives in nearby Pittsford, New York. His 22 Greenhaven and Lucent books include *Understanding the Adventures of Huckleberry Finn*, *Readings on J. K. Rowling*, *Violence in Suzanne Collins's The Hunger Games*, and *Global Viewpoints on the Internet*. He is the father of two children, Michael and Mollie Wiener, and is married to fabric artist Iris Schifren Wiener.